Emily Windsnap and the Monster from the Deep

LIZ KESSLER

illustrations by SARAH GIBB

CANDLEWICK PRESS

Text copyright © 2004 by Liz Kessler
Illustrations copyright © 2004 by Sarah Gibb

First published in Great Britain in 2004 by Orion Children's Books,
a division of the Orion Publishing Group

First U.S. paperback edition 2007

The Library of Congress has cataloged the hardcover edition as follows:

Kessler, Liz.
Emily Windsnap and the monster from the deep / Liz Kessler ;
illustrations by Sarah Gibb. — 1st U.S. ed.
p.   cm.
Summary: Reunited with her merman father and now living on an island located in the Bermuda Triangle, twelve-year-old Emily accidentally awakens the fearsome kraken and also faces a bully from her past.
ISBN 978-0-7636-2504-7 (hardcover)
[1. Mermaids — Fiction. 2. Monsters — Fiction. 3. Bullies — Fiction.
4. Neptune (Roman deity) — Fiction.]   I. Gibb, Sarah, ill. II. Title.
PZ7.K4842Emi 2006
[E] — dc22   2005054261

ISBN 978-0-7636-3301-1 (first paperback edition)
ISBN 978-0-7636-6018-5 (second paperback edition)

12 13 14 15 16 17 RRC 10 9 8 7 6 5 4 3 2

Printed in Crawfordsville, IN, U.S.A.

This book was typeset in Bembo.

Candlewick Press
99 Dover Street
Somerville, Massachusetts 02144

visit us at www.candlewick.com

Below the thunders of the upper deep;

Far far beneath in the abysmal sea,

His ancient, dreamless, uninvaded sleep

The Kraken sleepeth . . .

from "The Kraken,"
by Alfred, Lord Tennyson

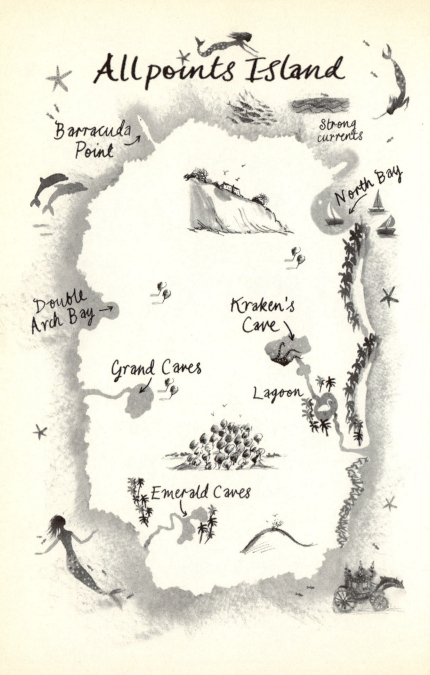

Allpoints Island

Barracuda Point

Strong currents

North Bay

Double Arch Bay

Kraken's Cave

Grand Caves

Lagoon

Emerald Caves

Chapter One

*C*lose your eyes.

Think of the most beautiful place you can imagine.

Are you seeing golden beaches? Gorgeous clear blue sea? Perfect sky? Keep your eyes closed.

Now multiply that by about a hundred, and you're halfway to picturing what my new home is like. The softest, whitest sand, palm trees that reach lazily out from the beaches, tall rocky arches cusping the bays, sea that sparkles like crystals in the sunlight. All thanks to Neptune, the ruler of the ocean.

He sent me here with my mom and dad to start a new life. Somewhere we could live together. Somewhere our secret would be safe.

One of Neptune's guards, Archieval, accompanied us here. He's a merman. He swam beside our little sailboat, *King,* all the way, swishing his long black hair behind him and occasionally ducking under, flicking his tail in the air, silver and sharp, like a dagger.

We edged slowly into a horseshoe-shaped bay filled with shiny turquoise water. Soft foamy waves gently stroked the white sand. A few boats were dotted about in the bay, half-sunken, silently sloping. Some were modern yachts, others great wooden crafts that looked like ancient pirate ships.

A tall rocky arch marked the end of the bay. Through it, the sand and sea continued around a corner. I caught my breath as I stood and stared.

"Shake a tail, someone," Archieval called up. "I could use some help here."

I leaned across to help him pull the boat alongside a wooden jetty as Dad swam around to the back and tied the ropes to a buoy. Mom was still inside with Millie. That's her friend from Brightport. Millie used to read fortunes on the pier. She did a tarot reading for Archieval before we left, and he liked it so much, he invited her to come with us. They had to check with Neptune first, but Archieval is one of Neptune's top guards, so he's pretty much allowed to do as he likes.

Then Millie said she'd have to let the cards decide, so she set the pack out in a star shape and sat looking at it in silence for about ten minutes, nodding slowly.

"Well, it's obvious what I have to do. You'll never catch me ignoring a call from the ten of cups," she said enigmatically before throwing her black cape over her shoulder and going home to pack her things. Millie says everything enigmatically. I've learned to just nod and look as though I know what she's talking about.

Archieval swam around to the side of the boat. "This is it, then," he said. "North Bay, Allpoints Island."

"Why's it called Allpoints Island?" I asked.

"It's right in the center of the Triangle." He stretched out an arm as he spun slowly around in a circle. "Where the three points meet."

The Bermuda Triangle. I shivered. He'd told us about it on the way here, about the boats and planes that had mysteriously disappeared inside it. An ocean liner had been found totally intact but utterly deserted. Twenty tables were set out for dinner. Another ship was found with skeletons on the decks, its sails ripped to shreds all around them. Others had vanished without a trace, often after frantic mayday calls from pilots and fishermen who were never seen again.

I didn't know whether to believe the stories at first, but something had happened out at sea. We'd been sailing along normally, the swells rising and falling, the boat gently making its way through the peaks and troughs. Then it changed. The water went all glassy. The engine cut out; everything died. Even my watch stopped working. It felt as if the sea had frozen, almost as if time itself had frozen.

Then Archieval yanked his long hair into a ponytail with some string and disappeared under the water. A few minutes later, we got moving again, gliding silently across the glassy sea.

"That was it," he called up. "Bermuda Triangle. That's what'll protect you from the outside world now. No one knows how to get through it except for a few chosen merfolk." He threw a rope onto the deck. "Well, a few chosen merfolk and . . . no, I'd better not tell you about that."

"What? Tell me."

Archie beckoned me closer. "I shouldn't really tell you this," he said, "but there's a raging current down there. Not any normal kind of current either, oh no. This one's linked to something that lies deep down in the sea, even below your island."

"What? What is it?"

"What is it? It's the biggest, scariest, most powerful—"

"I hope you're not filling my daughter's head with any more of your lurid tales, Archie!" Dad said, suddenly turning up beside Archie. "She has enough nightmares as it is."

I'd told Dad all about my nightmares on the way here, the ones I used to have in Brightport: swimming around in a fish tank surrounded by my old classmates, all shouting "Freak! Freak!" at me, or being chased by a scientist with a big net.

How many more nightmares was I going to have? Would I get to leave them behind? Would I ever stop feeling like the odd one out?

Archie lowered his voice. "Just be careful," he said. "That glassy plane marks out the Triangle, but it's only like that on the surface. It's a huge well below, leading down to the deepest depths of the ocean. And you don't want to go disappearing down a hole like that."

I rubbed the goose bumps crawling up my arms.

We'd sailed on calmly after that, slipping through water that grew clearer and lighter every moment, melting from deep navy to a soft baby blue. I tried to push Archie's words to the back of my mind.

Gradually, the island came into view. It was quite small, perhaps only a few miles across: a tall cliff at one end, a couple of lower peaks at the other, and a low, flat stretch in between. As we drew closer, I could see that the coastline was made up of long white bays fringed with tall palm trees and clusters of rocks and arches. It looked like a postcard. I'd always thought those pictures must be made up somehow and that when you got there, you'd just find a clump of high-rise apartments next to a building site.

But it was real. And it was my new home.

"Where's your dad?" Mom joined me on the deck, straightening her skirt and bending down to check her reflection in a metal railing.

I pointed ahead. "Helping Archie."

Mom looked slowly around the bay. "I think I've died and gone to heaven," she murmured as she grabbed the railing. "Someone's going to have to pinch me."

"I'll do it!" Dad's head poked out of the water, a glint in his eyes as he wiped his floppy wet hair off his forehead. Mom smiled back at him.

A second later, the side doors crashed open and Millie clambered out. "Tell you something," she said, rubbing her large stomach. "That slippery elm mixture works wonders on seasickness." She covered her mouth as she hiccupped. "Especially washed down with a spot of brandy. Now, where are we?"

She squinted into the sunlight. "That's it!" she said, pointing across at a wooden ship lying on a slant in the bay. It had three tall masts, polished pine railings, and a name printed on the side: *Fortuna*.

"That's what?" I asked.

"Your new home. Archie told me."

I looked at Mom. "What's wrong with *The King of the Sea*?" That's our boat's full name. I've lived on it with Mom all my life.

Millie pinched my cheek as she squeezed past me. "Well, your dad can't live with you on a regular boat, can he now? Don't worry. I'll take care of the place for you."

Dad swam around to the side, staring across at *Fortuna*. "Flipping fins! A little different from where I've spent the last twelve years," he said as he reached up to help Mom off the boat. Dad was in prison before we came here. He's not a criminal or anything. Well, he broke the law, but it was a stupid law. He married a human. That's my mom. He's a merman. Makes it a little difficult when she can't swim and he can't go on land, but they manage somehow. She used to be a great

7

swimmer till she was hypnotized into being afraid of water. Neptune did that, to keep them apart. She's still nervous about it now, but Dad's started teaching her again.

Mom hitched up her skirt and stepped across onto the jetty. It led all the way out to the ship, bouncing and swaying on the water as we made our way along it.

I climbed aboard our new home. It was huge! At least twenty yards long with shiny brown wooden decks and maroon sails wrapped into three neat bundles. It lay perfectly still at a small tilt, lodged in the sand. It looked as if it had been waiting for us.

I stepped into the cabin in the middle of the boat and found myself in a kitchen with steps leading forward and behind. I tried the back way first. It led to a small cabin with a bed, a beanbag chair, and a polished wooden cupboard. Circles of wavy light bounced onto the bed from port-holes on either side. Definitely my bedroom!

I ran through to the other side. Mom was twirling around in a big open living room that had a table on one side and a comfy-looking sofa tucked snugly into the other.

"What will we do with all this space?" she gasped. Sunny golden rays beamed into the room from skylights all along the ceiling. Ahead, a door led to another bedroom.

"What about Dad?" I asked. "How's he going to live here?"

Before she had a chance to reply, a large trapdoor in the floor sprung open and he appeared below us. That was when I noticed there were trapdoors everywhere, leading down from each room into another one below. The ship was lodged in the seabed with a whole floor half-submerged, so you could swim around in it underwater.

"You want to see the rest of your new home?" Dad's eyes shone wide and happy.

I inched down through the trapdoor to join him. Almost as soon as I did, my legs started to tingle. Then they went numb. Finally, they disappeared altogether.

My tail had formed. Sparkling and glistening, it flickered into life, sending shimmery green and pink lights around me.

It does that when I go into water. Sometimes I'm a mermaid; sometimes I'm a girl. That's what happens when a woman and a merman have a baby.

I'd only found out recently, when I went swimming at school. Thinking about that first time made me tremble. In fact, the thought of Brightport Junior High made me feel sick even now. I'd started to dread going there. School itself didn't bother me, only some of the people. One in particular: Mandy Rushton. Just thinking about her was enough to make my skin prickle. All those times she'd made my life a misery. Like the time she pushed me into the pool in front of everyone. I almost gave the whole thing away, and would have if the teacher hadn't sent us both to get changed. I can still remember her icy cold tone of voice as she'd hissed at me on the way to the changing room. "I'll get you back for this, fish girl," she'd said. "Just wait."

I lived in fear of the day she'd get me. I'd have nightmares about it nearly every night, then I'd wake up, cold and sweaty, and have to face her all over again in real life.

At least I'd gotten her back in the end when I turned into a mermaid in the pool, right in front of her eyes. It was worth all the bullying just to see the look of stunned silence slapped across her face that day.

No, it wasn't. The only thing that made the bullying worth it was knowing I would never, ever have to see her again.

Bullies like Mandy Rushton were a thing of the past.

*　*　*

"A little bigger than *The King of the Sea,* eh?" Dad said as I lowered myself toward him. He took my hand, and we swam around the lower deck together. The feel of his big fingers closing around mine warmed something inside me and made up for the awkward silence between us. I couldn't think how to fill it.

"Look!" He pulled me through an archway in the center and through purple sea fans that hung like drapes from the ceiling. Fernlike and feathery, they swayed delicately with the movement of the water. Dad squeezed my hand.

A couple of red and white fish swam in through an empty porthole, pausing to nibble gently at the side of the boat before gliding between the drapes. One of them swam up to slide along Dad's tail. "Glasseye snappers," I said as he flicked it away. Dad smiled. He'd taught me the names of all sorts of fish on the way here. It was one of the few things we talked about. Where do you start after twelve years?

I swam back to the trapdoor and hoisted myself up. "Mom, it's amazing!" I said as I watched my tail form back into my legs. Mom stared. She obviously hadn't gotten used to it yet. She'd only seen it happen a few times.

Then Dad joined us and Mom turned to sit with her legs dangling over the trapdoor, gazing at him. He reached onto her lap to hold her hands. She didn't seem to notice that the bottom of her skirt was soaking wet. She just grinned stupidly down at him while he grinned stupidly up at her.

I realized I was grinning stupidly at both of them.

Well, most people don't have to wait till they're twelve before they get to see their parents together. I never knew it would make me feel so warm, so complete.

I decided to leave them to it. They wouldn't notice if I went out to explore. They'd hardly noticed anything except each other since we set off to come here! Not that I minded. After all, I'd nearly gotten imprisoned myself, getting them back together. I guessed they wouldn't mind a little time on their own.

"I'm going out for a while," I called. "Just for a look around."

"OK, darling," Mom replied dreamily.

"Be careful," Dad added.

I nearly laughed as I climbed out of the boat. I looked out at the turquoise water and marshmallow sand. Careful? What of? What could possibly hurt me here?

* * *

I walked along the beach for a while, watching the sun glint and dance on the water in between the ships. The sand was so white! Back home, or what used to be home, in Brightport, the sand was usually a dirty beige color. This sand was like flour. My feet melted into it as I walked. I could hardly feel the ground. A gentle breeze made the sun's warmth feel like a hair dryer on my body.

Wading into the sea, I couldn't help glancing around to check that I was alone. Just habit. I still hadn't gotten used to the idea that being a mermaid didn't make me a freak here—a secret island where merfolk and humans lived together. The only place of its kind in the world, protected by the magic of the Bermuda Triangle.

There were some people up on the cliff behind me, standing in front of a cluster of white buildings. For a moment, I considered scrambling up the hill to join them. Then I looked out at the water and saw faces—and then tails. Merpeople! I had to meet them! I pushed away a slight feeling of guilt as I turned away from the people—and toward the sea. It wasn't the human folk that interested me. It was the merpeople I wanted to meet!

As my legs formed back into my tail, I wondered if there were any others on the island like me. Half-human, half-merperson. That would be *so* cool! Either way, at least I could live here with my mom and dad without us having to hide what we are.

Shoals of tiny fish escorted me out toward the group, gliding and weaving around me. With thin black bodies and see-through fins, they led me along through the warm water, slowing down every now and then, almost as though they were making sure I could keep up. Wavy lines rippled along the seabed like tire tracks. A troop of silver jacks swam past me in a line, each one silhouetted against the sand below, their shadows doubling their gang's number.

I flipped over onto my back, flicking my tail every now and then to propel myself lazily along, until I remembered I was supposed to be looking for the merpeople.

I stopped and looked around. The island was a speck in the distance, miles away. How long had I been swimming?

The merpeople had moved on. A chill gripped my chest as I realized I was gliding over some dark rocks: hard, gray, jagged boulders with plants lining every crack. Fat gray fish with wide-open mouths and spiky backs glared at me through cold eyes. Long trails of seaweed stretched like giant snakes along the seabed, reaching upward in a clutch of leaves and stems.

As I hovered in the water, I could feel myself being pulled along by a current. It felt like a magnet, drawing me toward it, slowly at first, then getting stronger. I swam hard against it, but it was too strong. It was reeling me in like a fishing line. Blackness swirled ahead of me. Then I remembered. The Triangle.

Everything sped up, like a film on fast forward. Fish zoomed past, weeds and plants lay horizontally, stretched out toward the edge of the Triangle, the well that led to the deepest depths of the ocean.

My chest thumping, my throat closing up, I worked my arms like rotary blades, pounding through the water. My tail flicked rapidly as I fought to get away. I swam frantically. *Keep going, keep going!*

But every time I started to make progress, the current latched on to me again, dragging me back out to sea. We were locked in a battle, a tug of war between me and—and what? The biggest, scariest—what? What hadn't Archie told me? What was down here? I could almost feel it, a kind of vibration or humming. Was I imagining it? Fear surged through me like an electric current, powering my aching arms for one final push.

It was just enough. I was getting away. The current loosened its grip. The sea soon became shallow again, and calm, as though nothing had happened. But I wasn't taking any risks. Catapulting myself through the water, I swam back to our bay and made it to the ship, breathless. I pulled myself out and sat panting on the deck while my tail disappeared and my legs re-formed.

Mom poked her head out of the cabin. "You OK, sweetie?" she asked, handing me a towel.

I nodded, too out of breath to reply. I rubbed myself dry as I followed her back into the kitchen.

"Here y'are," she said, passing me a couple of onions and a knife. "Might as well make yourself useful." Then she looked at me more carefully. "Are you sure you're all right?"

Was I? That was a good question. I opened my mouth to answer her, but stopped when I heard voices coming from below deck.

"Who's that?"

"Oh, visitors, downstairs with your dad. They've been coming all afternoon."

I gently shut the trapdoor. I couldn't face new people yet. I didn't even want Dad to hear what I had to say. I don't know why. Something to do with how happy he was, and the fact that he kept giving me all these smiley, loving looks. Well, he would do that, wouldn't he? He hadn't seen me since I was a baby. And I didn't want him to know his baby wasn't quite so happy right now, or quite so sure about this new dream home of hers. I mean, sure, it was beautiful and everything. But there was something else going on here. I didn't know what it was; just a sense of something lurking, or lying in wait.

My hands shook as I started to peel the onions. "Mom," I said carefully.

"Mm?" she replied through a teaspoon lodged in her mouth. She says it keeps her eyes from watering.

"You know that stuff Archie told us on the way here, about the big well in the ocean?"

"Buh big well im be oshug?" she replied, the spoon waggling about as she spoke.

"What?"

She pulled the spoon out of her mouth. "The big well in the ocean?" she repeated.

"The one that leads to the deepest depths of the ocean," I added as a shudder snaked through my body. "I felt something just now. Pulling me out to sea."

"Emily, you're not to go out there!" she said, grabbing my arms. "You stay close to the island."

The shudder jammed in my throat. "It was really strong, Mom," I said quietly.

"Of course it's really strong! It's protecting the whole area! You know what Archie said. Do you hear me, Emily?"

I nodded, swallowing hard. "Yes, I hear you."

"I'm not going to lose you, Emily. You promise me you'll keep away from there." She stared at me, holding my eyes with hers. I could see fear in them, and I was about to tell her I was fine and not to worry. Then I remembered what she'd already been through with me, how she'd followed me when I went out to sea to find my dad, and how Neptune nearly locked us all in prison. I guess she had the right to worry a little.

"I promise," I said.

She pulled me toward her and hugged me tight. "Good. Right," she said. "You silly thing, you're shaking." She squeezed me tighter. "Come on, it's OK. Let's get these veggies done, and we'll try not to think about big wells and the deepest depths of the ocean, OK?"

"OK." I forced a smile. "I'll try."

We worked in silence after that. I couldn't think of anything to say. All I could think was that it would take more than chopping a few onions to make me forget the fear I'd felt out there, clutching and snapping at me like a shark trying to drag me to the bottom of the sea.

18

Mermaids? Yeah, right!

You're as bad as my dad.

He thinks they're real, too. Thinks he's seen one. He says it was on his way back from The Fisherman. That's our local bar. Clear as day, he says.

"Well, that goes to show how reliable your vision is after ten beers," my mom says. "You couldn't even tell it was the middle of the *night*!"

"Clear as day," he says again. "It's just an expression, love."

Mom says he'll be seeing more than mermaids if he doesn't start pulling his weight. Then she gets mad at me for leaving my *Girltalk* magazine lying around. That's the only time she seems to notice me nowadays, when she's nagging me about something. And Dad wouldn't know if I disappeared altogether—he's hardly ever around.

It wasn't always like this. Just ever since we heard that the town council is planning to pull down our home. We live on a pier and they say it's not safe. The problem is, my parents work on the pier, too. So that's job and home gone in one swift swing of a crane. Or blast of dynamite. However they do it.

The place is a dump, anyway. I don't care what happens. Well, OK, maybe I do. But who cares what I think? I wish they did.

So today, Dad charges upstairs at lunchtime. He usually goes to the bar, but he says he's been somewhere else.

"Where?" Mom eyes him suspiciously.

"Look," he says. He's got a magazine in his hand. A brochure.

Mom takes it from him. *"Mermaid Tours?"* she says. "Oh, for Lord's sake, Jack, when will you grow up?"

"No, it's not—it's not—" he blusters. "It's just the name of the company, Maureen. It caught my attention, that's all." He grabs the brochure back from Mom and rifles through it as though he's looking for something in particular. "I've been looking for something to take our minds off everything. I thought this might help.

"There!" he says suddenly, opening it up and slamming it onto the table. Mom sits down to read it. I have a look, too. Not that I'm interested or anything. I just want to know what the fuss is about, that's all.

"A cruise, Jack?" Mom looks at him in this way she has, with her tongue in her cheek and her eyebrows raised so high they nearly disappear into her hair. "We're on the verge of losing our livelihood and you want us to spend every last penny we haven't even GOT on some ridiculous vacation!"

Dad takes a deep breath. "Maureen," he says in a rumble. When he speaks again, he says each word on its own, like he's talking staccato. "What. Kind. Of. Fool. Do. You. Take. Me. For. Exactly?"

Mom gets up from the table. "You really don't want me to answer that, Jack."

"Mom, please don't—" I start. But what's the point? She doesn't reply, doesn't even look at me. I might as well not be here.

Hello! I am here, you know. I matter!

"Look!" Dad suddenly shouts. Dad never shouts. We both look. He's pointing at the page. "I'll read it to you, shall I?" And before we have time to answer, he starts reading.

"Enter our EXCLUSIVE contest, and you could win one of our superlative MERMAID TOURS vacations! Every month, one lucky reader will win this FANTASTIC PRIZE. Just complete the following phrase in thirty words or less: 'Mermaid Tours are the best vacations around because . . .'

Remember to tell us which of our fabulous cruise vacations you'd like to go on, and mail the coupon to us. You could be our next lucky winner!"

Dad puts the magazine back on the table.

"Well," Mom says, picking up the magazine. "A contest. Why didn't you just say so?"

I roll my eyes at Dad. He clamps his jaw shut and doesn't say anything.

Mom and Dad are complete fanatics about contests, especially Mom. She thinks she's got a system. It works, too. Our home is littered with teddy bears and toasters and electronic dictionaries she's won from stupid contests in magazines. We had three vacuum cleaners at one point. She even won a weekend getaway once. Not that I know much about that. She and Dad went without me. I had to stay at home with a babysitter while they went off to live it up in New York.

I'll admit it, all right: it was the loneliest weekend of my life. I mean, so the prize was a vacation for two, but couldn't they at least have asked if they could bring their daughter? Would it have hurt so much for the thought to have crossed their minds?

But this. Well, this is for all of us. And I wouldn't mind a cruise vacation. Lying on a lounge chair on an enormous ship gliding through the ocean, hot sun, warm pool, all the food I can eat, nonstop desserts, and no one to stop me from drinking as much soda as I want. I've heard about these vacations. It's all included.

"You know how good you are at these things," Dad says, edging closer to Mom.

"Don't try flattery, Jack," Mom says. "It doesn't suit you."

But I know she'll do it; she can't resist. I catch Dad's eye. He winks, and I half smile back. Well, he's still stupid, believing in mermaids.

Later that day, I see Mom leafing through the brochure. "Look at this one," she says. I glance over her shoulder.

Bermuda and the Caribbean. Experience the magic for yourself. Enjoy all the comfort and enchantment of our Mermaid Tours cruise. Swim with dolphins. Bask in year-round sunshine heaven.

"That's the one, I'd say." She nibbles the side of her mouth. "OK, leave me alone now. I need to think."

She won't show either of us what she's written. Says it'll jinx it. But something changes around the place after she's sent it off. Mom and Dad get along; they even smile at each other occasionally.

We all start talking about what we'll do on our cruise and what it'll be like. All of us, all in it together—it feels great! For a few days. The contest ends in a week.

But then the week's up, and we don't hear anything. Another week passes, and another, and another. Nothing.

We haven't won. Mom's luck's run out after all.

And gradually, the sniping at each other starts again, and the being so wrapped up in themselves that they forget to think about me. Back to normal. And underneath it all is the looming truth that no one's saying out loud, that we're about to lose everything.

Well, why should I expect anything different? It is *my* life we're talking about here.

Oh, I haven't told you my name yet, have I?

It's Mandy. Mandy Rushton.

Chapter Two

I jumped out of bed. Shona was arriving today!

Shona's my best friend. She's a mermaid. Full-time. Not just when she goes in water, like me. Back home—I mean, back in Brightport—I used to sneak out at night to meet up with her. That was before anyone knew about me being a mermaid. Now we could see each other every day!

I couldn't believe it when she said they were coming too. It was Neptune's idea, but I'd never met her parents and didn't know if they'd agree to it. Mind you, looking around me, it was hard to imagine anyone not wanting to come to live here. As long as you didn't go anywhere near the edge of the Triangle. Or think about what might be down there, under the island . . .

Well, I wasn't going to think about that today. I'd stick close to the coast, like Mom said, and everything would be all right. It all looked different this morning anyway. Nothing this beautiful could be dangerous. I'd gotten it all out of proportion yesterday. Like my old teacher used to say, I've got a good imagination.

Dad swam up to the trapdoor in the living room as I was getting some breakfast. "There's someone here for you, little 'un," he said. "And look, I got you something."

He darted away as someone else appeared below me. Someone with long blond hair and a big smile. Shona!

I shoveled a last spoonful into my mouth and jumped down through the trapdoor with a splash. My legs melted away, turning into a tail.

"I couldn't wait to see you," Shona said, swimming toward me to hug me tight.

I hugged her back. "When did you get here?"

"Late last night." She nodded toward the porthole she'd swum through. "Althea brought me over to North Bay. She lives next door to us at Rocksea Cove. Come and meet her."

"Oh. Great," I said. I wasn't going to have

Shona all to myself then? But there was so much to catch up on! Well, I suppose we'd find time soon—and at least I was going to meet another mermaid.

"Here you are." Dad swam back over, smiling broadly as he held something out to me. A doll. It had bright red spots on its cheeks, golden hair, and a frilly pink tail.

"Um. Thanks, Dad."

"You like it?" he asked, anxiously tugging at his ear.

"Sure. I'll play with it later, perhaps."

"I wanted to give you something like this years ago. I've been saving it," he said, his eyes going all misty and dreamy. They seemed to do that a lot. I don't know if he realized I was nearly thirteen. "I mean, I know it's a bit childish, but . . ."

"No, it's fine, Dad. It's great. Thanks."

Once we were outside, I grimaced at Shona, and she laughed. Then I had a pang of guilt. "Hang on," I said. I swam back in to the boat and kissed Dad on the cheek. It isn't his fault I grew up without him. It isn't his fault we haven't worked out how to communicate with each other yet, either. It will come. It has to. I mean, it's great being with him, but we've hardly had a real conversation. It feels as if we don't quite know how to at times.

"What's that for?" he asked, lifting his hand to his cheek.

I shrugged, smiling briefly. "See you later," I said.

Outside the boat, a mergirl with jet black hair tied back in a ribbon was waiting in the water with Shona. The ribbon looked as if it was made out of gold seaweed. Her tail was green, with silver stars painted on the end.

Shona turned to me. "This is Althea. She's going to show us around the island."

"Great," I said with a tight smile as a pang of jealousy hit me. How could I compete with a full-time, real mermaid with stars on her tail and gold seaweed in her hair? I was going to end up without a best friend again.

"We're picking up Marina first," Althea said.

"That's Althea's best friend," Shona added, laughing as she swam ahead with Marina. I think she was trying to put my mind at rest. So why didn't it work?

"Stay close to the coast here," Althea warned as we set off, doubling the fear that was already starting to gnaw at my insides. "There's quite a current around the northern end of the island."

As if I needed to be told that! I couldn't speak. My mouth was so dry it felt like it had sand in it.

Althea pointed to the hill behind us. "That's where a couple of the human families live," she said, pointing up at the white buildings I'd seen the day before. "They take care of gardens for the whole island."

For a moment I wished I'd gone up to meet them yesterday after all. If I had, maybe I'd be looking around at everything with wide innocent eyes like Shona was doing now, instead of waiting for something awful to happen. But then, if I had, Althea and Marina might not be interested in me. They wouldn't want a human hanging around with them. And surely Shona wouldn't either. No, it was the mermaids I wanted to be with. I was one of them now, and that's how it was going to stay.

I linked Shona's arm with mine and smiled at her. Swimming on, I made sure we stayed as close to the shore as possible.

We followed a low line of rocks that jutted into the ocean. "That's Barracuda Point," Althea said.

"Why's it called that?" Shona asked.

"You'll see," she said with a smile. "Wait till we're on the other side."

We rounded the tip and swam on a little farther before Althea stopped. "OK, look now."

We turned and looked back.

"Sharks alive!" Shona gasped. I stared in silence. A low line of rocks twisted out from the shore, stretching out into a long thin body. At the tip, it narrowed into a sharp point, dented and creased along the middle, like a jawline filled with sharp teeth. Jagged rocks stood along the top like fins. Dark and menacing, it looked as though it could easily come to life with a snarling twist of its body. A cold shiver darted up my spine, prickling into my neck.

"It's supposed to protect the island," Althea said.

"What from?"

"Everything. There's all sorts of bogey-mers lurking, you know."

"Really?" I asked, shivering. "Like what?"

Althea laughed. "It's just kids' stories. Monsters and stuff." Then she stopped smiling. "But there's something to them, I think. I've never been able to quite put my fin on it, but I've always had a sense of something . . . something below the surface."

"Me too! Have you ever been pulled out to sea?" I blurted out before I could stop myself.

"What?"

"By—by the current," I faltered.

"We avoid certain spots. We learn very quickly about that."

"And what happens if you don't?" I asked, holding my breath while I waited for her to answer.

Althea lowered her voice. "The bogey-mer will get you!" she said. Then she looked at my face and burst out laughing. "Come on, I'm only joking. It's kids' tales, like I said." Then she turned suddenly, shaking her hair so it splashed onto the water, spreading golden droplets in an arc around her. "Come on. Let's go and get Marina."

She moved on. As we swam, Shona gave me an occasional sideways look. I smiled at her and tried to act casual, but my body felt stiff and clumsy as I pushed myself through the sea. I couldn't shake the feeling that I just wasn't as good at all this as they were. It didn't come as naturally. I mean, up until a few months ago, I'd never even been in water! My cheeks flushed as I prayed Shona would never tell anyone that.

The water soon became warm and shallow and colorless as we skirted the island. No currents, nothing weird. Althea was right. We just had to avoid certain spots and everything would be fine. I began to relax. We came to a wide bay. As we swam into it, the water turned cool and deep. Twisted rock formations stood along the edges.

31

"Double Arch Bay," Althea said.

Ahead of us, two giant arches were cut deep into the rocky shore. Althea ducked under to swim through one of them. Shona went next. Then I flicked myself down and slipped through.

We swam across a small reef. Neat clusters of plants and coral were dotted about, making it like a well-tended park. An elderly merman with shiny blue eyes and a thin gray tail swam across them, snipping at weeds with a knife made from razor shells.

"Hi, Theo," Althea said.

He nodded at us. "Morning, girls."

"Theo's the gardener," Althea explained as he swam off to tie some wilting pink plants into a bundle with seaweed.

There were archways everywhere. Some were tiny gaps in the rocks that I'd have missed if Althea hadn't pointed them out, others wide jagged holes big enough for a whale to get through.

Eventually, we came to a shimmery purple rock with a neat round hole in the middle. "This is where Marina lives," Althea said. She tapped a pink fish hovering at the entrance, a gold bell dangling from its tail. Immediately, it wriggled its body and a delicate sound chimed.

A mermaid swam toward us from inside. She had curly red hair and a long gold tail with a shiny crescent moon painted on the end. "You must be Shona and Emily!" she said, her freckled face creasing into a smile. "Come in while I get my things." She grabbed Althea's hand and they went on ahead, along a narrow pathway lined with rough walls. It soon widened out into a wide living space divided up by trails of fern and kelp. An older mermaid bustled past us. She had red hair like Marina's, only hers was longer and frizzy. Her tail was bright yellow and tapered into soft white tassels at the end.

"Don't be out all day, Marina," she said. "It's jellied eel soufflé tonight and we're eating early. I've got my synchro swim class at seven." Then she smiled at Shona and me. "Hello, girls," she added. "Welcome to Allpoints Island."

Shona and I smiled back before following the others into a small space with a soft seaweed bed and drapes all around it. A huge pink sponge was squashed into one corner, a crystal mirror in another.

"My room," Marina said.

I sat on the sponge. It squelched and bubbled under me. Shona laughed. "It's swishy!"

Swishy—that's Shona's word for *everything* she likes. "Squishy, more like," I said as I tried to get up.

Althea swam toward the entrance. "Come on," she said. "There's loads to show you."

Marina grabbed a patchwork bag made of leaves and reeds and followed Althea, with Shona close behind. I fumbled my way out of the sponge and caught up with them as they slithered through the arches and back out into the bay. We swam along stretches of rocky coastline, interspersed with coves of all shapes and sizes: some wide and sandy, others tiny winding channels you could almost miss.

Everywhere we looked, spots of sunlight bounced on the water, white foamy waves washed gently over rocks, and palm trees reached gently out from marshmallow sand. High on the island, some people called down to us from a woody hill. In the sea, merfolk smiled and greeted us as we passed them. A couple of young mer-children riding piggyback on a dolphin waved and shouted to us. We waved back. A group of mermen diving for food nodded at us on their way out to sea. A mermaid with long flowing hair streaming down her back smiled as she was pulled along by a swordfish on a leash.

It was all so different—and yet so familiar. I belonged here. The fear that had gripped me since yesterday floated further away with every new sight.

Swimming on, we approached a half-hidden

cave in the rocky shoreline. "There are loads of caves on the island, but we only use a couple of them," Marina said. "School's in one of them. The other's only for really major events, like when Neptune comes. That's the Grand Caves. We can show you the other one, though, Emerald Caves. You want to see your school?"

Did I? Just the thought of school washed the smile off my face. But surely this couldn't be anything like Brightport Junior High. No one was going to make fun of me here or delight in making my life a misery. And it *was* a mermaid school! A mix of emotions and questions swirled around inside me as I followed Althea into the cave. It wouldn't happen again, would it? It couldn't; I'd make sure of it. I'd do everything I could to show the mermaids I was just like them.

We inched along a narrow tunnel. As it twisted and turned, it grew darker and darker. Soon we were swimming in pitch-blackness.

"Feel your way along the walls," Marina called from somewhere ahead of me. I ran my fingers along the craggy layered sides as I edged down the tunnel.

Just as my eyes were getting used to the dark, the tunnel opened out and grew lighter. We came to a fork.

"Down here." Marina pointed along a tunnel that shimmered with green light.

It led up into a deep pool inside the cave. Above us, the ceiling stretched high and jagged. Stalactites hung all around us: enormous pillars reaching almost to the water, tiny spindles spiking down like darts. Rocks glimmered and shone purple and blue and red. Next to the pool, smooth boulders were dotted about on the gravelly ground like an abandoned game of giants' marbles.

A long scroll hung from the ceiling, pictures of underwater life drawn all over it, a pile of different-colored reeds underneath.

A young mermaid was cleaning some hairbrushes lined up on a rocky ledge that jutted across the water. She smiled at us as we gazed around.

"Swishy!" Shona said, swimming over to the hairbrushes. "You have Beauty and Deportment?"

Beauty and Deportment. Shona had told me all about that. I'd be studying it with her soon. And Diving and Dance, and all the other mermaid subjects. No more long division!

"Of course," Marina smiled. "It's my favorite subject."

"Mine, too," Shona breathed.

Althea looked at me. "I prefer Shipwreck Studies."

I tried to think of something to say, to join in the conversation. But it was all so new and alien to me. They'd all been studying these subjects for years. What if I was no good at them?

"Althea likes going out on Geography Reef Trips," Marina said with a laugh. "Anything to get out of doing her tides tables."

"It's beautiful," Shona whispered as we took it all in. "Much better than my old school."

"And about a million light years away from mine," I added, trying not to think too hard about Brightport Junior High.

"There are two classes," Althea explained. "This one's for the older kids. There's another one for the babies."

"Two classes?" Shona asked. "Is that all?"

"There's only about thirty families here alto-gether," Marina said. "Mostly mer-families and a few human ones."

"Do they mix?" I asked. I realized I was hold-ing my breath while I waited for the reply.

"Yes, of course," Althea said as she started swimming back out of the cave. "But they're kind of separate, too." She blushed. "If you get what I mean." She glanced quickly at my tail. I got what she meant. I was the only one. Still the odd one out.

The old fears resurfaced, hitting me like a

punch in my stomach. I couldn't keep them away any longer. I'd *never* find a place where I could fit in.

"But everyone gets along really well," Marina said quickly, swimming across to touch my arm. "And we're all really pleased you've joined us. The island's organizing a party for you next week, once you've settled in."

"We haven't had any new families here for ages," Althea added. "Come on, let's show you the rest of the island."

They were organizing a party, just for us? Maybe I was wrong. Maybe things would work out, after all.

We continued around the coast, Althea and Marina pointing out sights all along the way: a hole in the ground that spouted orange flames in the summer, little channels leading to a maze of caves and caverns where some of the merfolk ran craft stalls. I made a mental note to tell Dad about that. At least it could be something for us to talk about. He'd learned to make jewelry while he was in prison. Maybe he could get one of the stalls.

Swimming up the jagged east side of the island, we came to a channel leading into the rock.

"Now this is something you must see," Althea said.

We set off in single file along the channel. The sides became steeper and higher as we swam; the water grew deeper and colder, and so dark it was almost black. A soft wind whistled through the chasm. Then nothing. No movement, no sound, the sun beating silently down. I'd never experienced such stillness. It felt as though it was inside me, as though it was part of me. For a moment, there was nothing except me and the stillness, silently winding through my body like a snake. Was it a pleasant feeling? I couldn't even tell.

I shivered and shook myself. The others had swum ahead—again. I tried not to show them how tired it was making me to keep up. And I decided not to mention the weird snakelike feeling either. Somehow I didn't think it would help me come across as normal.

As we wound our way along the channel, Althea and Marina kept pointing things out in our path: a fossil on the canyon wall, hairline cracks in the rocks making tiny channels that split off from the main one.

"Look." Althea pointed ahead, to where the

channel seemed to come to an end. I couldn't see anything at first, just a lot of overgrown bushes and reeds lining the walls. Then I noticed what she was pointing at. A gap in the rock, through the reeds. There were pieces of driftwood attached to either side of the gap, covered in plants and algae.

We parted the reeds as though they were curtains and peered through the gap in the rock. On the other side, a shimmering blue lagoon sparkled with diamond glints. The water lay virtually still; green ferns hung down across gaping holes in the rock; a group of flamingos gathered at the edge, standing motionless on spindly legs, their long pink necks stretched straight and high. Two pelicans flew past, their wings reaching wide as they skimmed the water's still surface.

It was like paradise. How you've always imagined paradise would look.

"Swishy!" breathed Shona.

I stared so hard my eyes watered.

Marina looked nervous. "Come on. We need to get back."

"But we just got here," I said.

"We shouldn't be here at all."

"We're not really supposed to," Althea said, swimming closer and lowering her voice. "But *you* don't know that. You could go in and find out what it's like. I've always wanted to know."

I stared at the lagoon.

"I'm not sure," Shona said. "I mean, if we're not allowed . . ."

"None of the kids is brave enough. We've been told not to go in there so many times," Althea said. "But you haven't. You've only been here five minutes! Who's going to tell you off?"

"She's right," I said.

Althea smiled at me. "Exactly," she said.

This could be just what I needed! My chance to make sure Althea and Marina would definitely accept me. If I did this, they'd have to see me as one of them. That was it, I'd decided. I was going to do it. I wasn't going to be whispered about and made fun of again. And I *wasn't* going to be the odd one out. This was my chance to make sure of it.

Besides, it looked *so* tempting in there. I could almost feel it inviting me in, beckoning me in, almost pulling me. What was it? Was I imagining that, too?

Shona edged away from the reeds, her tail fluttering nervously. "Let's think about it," she said.

We dropped the reeds and drew back, but I couldn't get the image out of my mind. The stillness of the water, the ferns hanging down like delicate chains. And more than that, the chance to seal my place as one of the mermaids. I had to do it—but I wasn't brave enough to do it on my own. I would have to persuade Shona.

We set off in silence. All around us, nature bustled. Tiny brown lizards raced across rocks. Crabs scuttled under large stones, sneaking into the safety of their hidden homes. Above us, white birds with long sharp tails pecked at the cliff, disappearing into invisible holes in the rock. Eventually, the channel's walls widened once more and the sun warmed our necks as we arrived back at the open ocean.

When the others left us, Shona came to North Bay with me. I grabbed her before we went into the boat. "We've got to go back," I said.

"Oh, Emily, I don't know," Shona said. "I mean, we've only just gotten here."

"That's the whole point!" I said. "Like Althea said, we're new, we don't know our way around, it would be *easy* for us to get lost. Think how impressed they'll be. Please!"

Shona half smiled. "It did look amazing," she murmured. "And I suppose we haven't really had long enough to properly understand the rules yet."

"Not long enough at all," I said, my tail flicking with excitement, and something more than that. A need, almost a hunger. "We're just having a look around our new home. We're curious, we're a little vague about directions, and—whoops— we've gone the wrong way. No one will be upset with us."

I'm the first one to the door when the mail arrives. I flip through the pile: just more bills for Mom and Dad to argue about.

But there's something else. A letter in a shimmery pink envelope. I turn it over. *Mermaid Tours!*

"Mom! Dad!"

They're at the door in seconds.

"Oh, my God!" Mom says, snatching the letter from me. "Who's going to open it?" Her hands are shaking.

"You do it, love," Dad says. "You entered the contest." He holds my hands. I'm shaking, too.

"It's probably just some junk mail or something," Mom says, tearing at the envelope. "Let's not get excited."

She reads aloud. " 'Thank you for entering our contest. We are delighted to inform you that you have won our—' Jack!" Mom drops the letter and stares at Dad.

I pick the letter up and read on. " '. . . delighted to inform you that you have won our Bermuda-and-the-Caribbean cruise vacation. You and your family will spend two weeks aboard one of our luxury ships and experience all the delights of a Mermaid Tours vacation. Many congratulations and have a good trip!' "

For a second, there's silence. Then Mom grabs me and screams. She pulls me into a tight squeeze. She's jumping up and down. "We won! We won!" she yells. "We're going on vacation! Oh, my God, we won, we won!"

I jump up and down with her till I can hardly breathe. She's holding me too tight. I pull away. Mom grabs Dad around the neck and kisses him. Kisses him! I don't think she's done that for about five years.

It worked. She won us a vacation! Maybe they'll start getting along again and everything will be all right. For a couple of weeks, at least.

Wonder if anyone will notice I'm gone. Julia might. She's kind of my best friend, not that she acts like it. She never really wanted to be my best friend. She always preferred that Emily Windsnap. I was just someone to fall back on when Emily wasn't around. Julia was really upset that day when Emily didn't show up. What am I supposed to do? Turn my back on her? Well, Emily wasn't there and I was. So Julia and I are best friends now. Fair's fair.

I wonder what happened to Emily and her mom. It feels kind of weird without them. Not that I miss her or anything. No way. Just that, well, it's kind of quiet around here without her. Sometimes I find myself looking out to sea, wondering if they'll ever come back. Stupid, huh? I'm not saying I want them to, don't get me wrong. Just, I don't know, maybe it could have been different. I mean, if she hadn't gotten me into trouble last year when she told on me for cheating in the arcade, then I wouldn't have had to hate her. I wasn't even cheating; I was trying to help her. Trying to be nice. Taught me not to bother trying *that* again in a hurry. It never works. Better just to keep your mouth shut and not get your hopes up.

Anyway, we're out of here. We're going on a cruise!

Chapter Three

We swam side by side to begin with. Below us, occasional shoals of parrotfish and bright red snappers swept across the sandy bed. When the channel narrowed, I swam ahead, slinking along the silent passageway. The ground soon became uncluttered: clear golden sand beneath us, the sun shining down, almost directly above our heads. Two silhouetted mermaid figures gliding along below the surface, our shadows came and went, appearing briefly before suddenly growing distorted with the splash of a tail breaking the water's still surface.

We came to the curtain of reeds draped down the channel's walls and the algae-coated wooden plaques. That's when the feeling started inside me. I didn't know what it was. A quivery kind of sensation jiggling around in my stomach. Nervous. Waiting for something—and a feeling that there was something waiting for me, too. Trying not to let Shona see my quivering hands, I parted the curtain and looked through the hole in the wall. The water sparkled and fanned out into a wide lagoon. Ferns hung down over cracks and gaps in the walls. A white tropical bird flew into a hole behind me, its long tail disappearing into the rock. Nothing else moved. Shona stared.

I turned to her. "Ready?" My voice shook.

She broke her gaze to look at me. "Let's just get this over with."

I glanced around to check that no one had followed us, then I squeezed through the gap and swam into the lagoon. The sun burned down, heating my neck and dancing on the water. Its light rippled below us in wavy lines across the sea floor.

As we slid across the stillness, the water grew colder and murkier. When the lagoon narrowed back into a channel, I couldn't see my reflection swimming along below me anymore. The walls lining our trail had lost their hardness. They were like chalk. I stopped and scraped my finger down the side. I made myself focus on the walls, almost flicking a switch to turn off the nagging wordless worry in my mind. Rock crumbled in my hand. The channel walls stretched upward, cold and gray and deserted.

"Emily!" Shona was pointing at something ahead. An engraving on the wall: a perfect circle with a fountain spiraling out from the center. It looked like a pinwheel, full of energy, almost as tall as us. I had this weird feeling I knew the picture, recognized it. Had I seen it in a book? Dreamed about it? What *was* it?

"Look at *this*!" Shona had swum ahead while I stared at the engraving.

I joined her in front of some ferns loosely covering a hole in the rock. The hole disappeared below the surface. We dived down. Under the water, it was just big enough to swim into.

"Cool!" I grinned at her. A secret tunnel reaching into the rock! "Shona, we *have* to see what's in there."

She frowned.

"Althea and Marina will be *so* impressed. No one else has dared to do it." I hoped that would be enough to make her want to do it. I wasn't going to tell her it was so much more than that for me, that I was doing this to prove I was a real mermaid—not just to them, but to her, too. Before she had a chance to argue, I'd slithered into the slimy, echoey darkness. Eventually I heard her follow behind.

The winding tunnel led us deeper and deeper into dead rock: tight, cold, and claustrophobic, but gradually widening and growing brighter as we swam. Bit by bit, a growing circle of light opened up ahead of us.

We swam toward it, finally coming out into a dome-shaped space in the middle of the cave. A high ceiling rippled faintly with the water's reflection.

"I don't understand," Shona said, looking around. "What's that light?"

I shook my head as we swam all around the rocky edges. It seemed to be coming from under the water.

"Come on." I dived down. "That's our answer!" I gasped. The floor of the cave was absolutely littered with crystals and stones and gold, all shining so brightly I almost had to shield my eyes. I'd never seen jewels like these. Dazzling pink rocks with sharp white edges lay on the ground in a circle, joined together by a thin line of gold. In their center, a bright blue stone shaped like a rocket pointed up to the surface of the water.

"What in the ocean...?" Shona swam around and around the display, her mouth open, her eyes huge, shining with the reflection of the blue stone.

I looked around. There was more. Once we started looking, it seemed that stones and crystals covered the entire floor of the cave, packed and tucked into gaps in the rock all around us.

"Emily, I think we need to get back." A fat green angelfish hovered between us, its startled eyes staring into ours before it spun around and disappeared into a rocky crevice. "We've seen it now. We're not supposed to be here."

I stopped gazing around. Shona was right. "OK," I said. "Let's go back." We'd found the answer to Althea's and Marina's questions. The lagoon hid a cave filled with jewels. But why? It didn't make sense.

Shona turned immediately and started making her way back toward the tunnel. But then I noticed something on the cave's wall: a picture exactly like the engraving we'd seen earlier, only even bigger. It looked like a mosaic. I knew that shape—I was sure of it. And even though it didn't make any sense, I had this overwhelming feeling that it knew me too! As we got closer, I could see it was made out of jewels: a huge golden one in the center, oval shaped and about half as tall as me, with multicolored strands spinning outward from it. I put my hand out to touch it. It wobbled.

"Shona!"

"Come on." She kept swimming.

I pushed at the jewel. It was lodged in the rock, but only loosely. We could probably get it out. I *had* to try. There was a secret in here—I was sure of it. Something was drawing me on and I couldn't resist it.

"Shona!" I called again. "Just look at this."

She stopped swimming and turned.

"It's loose!" I pulled at it, edging my fingertips underneath to lever it up. "Help me."

She swam reluctantly back to me. "I thought we were—sharks alive!"

"You thought we were sharks?"

Shona stared at the mosaic. "What is it?"

"Help me get it out."

"You're pulling my tail, aren't you? We can't go around vandalizing the place!"

"We're not vandalizing anything. We'll put it back. Let's just see what's behind it." An image of Althea's and Marina's faces flickered across my mind, their eyes wide and impressed with my bravery. All the other mermaids crowding around me, wanting to be my friends, accepting me as one of them, not the odd one out, not the freak. This cave was going to change my life; I just knew it.

Shona sighed heavily, then reluctantly dug her fingers under the jewel, and we gradually levered it little by little out of its hole. A moment later, we were holding it between us. We lowered it to the ground and it plopped onto the seabed with a soft *thunk,* scattering a shower of sand in a swirl around us.

"Now what?" Shona stared down at it.

I swam up to the hole it had left behind and poked my head into it. Another tunnel. I grabbed Shona's arm, pointing into the blackness. "We *have* to go down there."

"We don't *have* to go anywhere!" Shona snapped.

"*Please!* Aren't you dying to know what's in there? Can't you feel it?" This wasn't even about Althea and Marina anymore. It was more like a thirst, or a magnet pulling me.

A magnet? My throat closed up as I remembered. . . . But it couldn't lead to the Triangle. We were in the middle of the island.

Shona peered into the tunnel. Her eyes sparkled against the reflection of the crystals. I could see the dilemma in them. "We just have a quick look, see what's there, and then we go home," she said eventually.

"Deal!"

We edged our way carefully into the hole,

slithering along in the silent dark. Me first, Shona following closely behind. The tunnel grew colder as we made our way deeper into the rock. The edges became craggy and sharp.

And then, without warning, it suddenly stopped. A dead end.

"Now what?" I called to Shona.

"We go back. We've looked. There's nothing here. And I'm not exactly surprised, or disappointed. Come on."

How could it suddenly end like that? I was *sure* it was leading somewhere. I felt around on the rock in front of me. It was different from the walls. Smoother. I inched my hands around it. Then I realized why it was different.

"Shona! It's a boulder!"

"What?"

"There's something blocking the tunnel. Look, it's different from the walls. Feel it."

Shona squeezed forward to touch the boulder.

I felt my way around its edges. "There's a crack all around it." It was almost the same shape as the crystal at the other end. "Maybe it'll come loose."

Shona looked at me.

"Let's just try."

"How do I let you talk me into all these things?" she said with another sigh.

"Because you can feel it, too? Because there's something down here that's making you tingle with excitement? Because the last time we went exploring, we ended up finding my dad? Because being my friend means you get to live on a beautiful desert island? Because—"

"OK, enough." Shona half frowned, half smiled. "Don't get your tail in a tizzy. Let's just get on with it."

Because I couldn't turn back now if I wanted to, even if I don't know why. I didn't say that part out loud, though.

It didn't just slip out like the jewel at the other end. We pushed and pushed, but nothing happened. Or nearly nothing. The boulder moved slightly, rocking backward and forward as though it was on a hinge, but we couldn't shift it.

"It's useless," Shona gasped. "We'll never get it out."

"We need to use the rocking. Get a momentum going. Look, it's swaying. If we both push it from above, it might topple. Wait till I say. On the count of three. You ready?"

Shona nodded without looking at me.

"One." I felt around for a good hold on the rock.

"Two." I stretched out my tail, getting ready to flick it as hard as I could.

"Three!"

We swished and pushed, grunting and heaving.

"Now, let go!" The rock swayed away from us, and then back. "And again." Another shove against the rock, another slight movement. Again and again, we heaved and pushed until, finally, it started to loosen.

Then Shona stopped pushing. "I've had enough. I'm exhausted."

"But we're nearly there!"

"I want to go back," she said. "I don't want to do this."

"What's the problem?"

"The *problem* is that we don't know what's on the other *side*!"

"Exactly! But there is something, isn't there? I can almost feel it vibrating in my body."

"Me too. And I don't like it, Em. It doesn't feel good. I don't want to know what it is, and I want to go before this place collapses in on us."

"It's just a boulder. It's not going to collapse!"

But Shona turned to go back.

"Just one more push."

"You do it if you like. I'm going."

"Fine!" I went back to the boulder. It was teetering on the edge of the hole now. I could probably push it on my own. I didn't even know why I was doing it anymore. I just knew there was something here. I could feel it. Low vibrations hummed rhythmically through the cave, and inside me, growing stronger. What *were* they?

Fueled by frustration, I spun my tail as fast as I could, pushed all my weight against the rock, and heaved.

Very slowly, it teetered, swaying with the rhythm of the water before eventually toppling: a huge, smooth, oval rock slipping down and away from us, almost in slow motion. Water swirled all around. The boulder was still traveling—rolling, hurtling down through the water.

It felt like when you roll a snowball down a hill and it grows bigger and bigger. Something was building up on the other side of the tunnel, below us, below the island, deep inside the rock. Nerve endings jangled and jammed like simmering explosions under my skin.

"I told you, I told you!" Shona screamed. "It's caving in! We're going to be trapped!"

"It's OK. Look." I tried to keep my nerve. Everything was still intact in the tunnel. It was just on the other side that the water was foaming and swirling everywhere. And there was something else: a presence. The vibrations had turned into a low rumbling, way down below. Something was down there. Something that didn't feel quite so exciting anymore. What was it? Images swirled around my mind: the mosaic, the spiral, whirling, spreading out, writhing.

"What's *happening*?" Shona screamed.

"It's just—it's the rock falling to the bottom of the caves," I said, much more confidently than I felt. "It's all right. Just stay calm. It'll stop in a minute."

The rock kept plummeting and crashing, getting fainter and fainter. Sand and rock particles swirled around, a few of them spinning softly through the hole into the cave.

And then it stopped. No more crashing. No swirling rocks or sand, no hurtling anywhere. Complete silence.

Total silence. Kind of eerie silence.

I smiled nervously at Shona. "See," I said. "Told you it'd all be OK."

And then we heard it. The rumbling. Not a flutter of excitement in our stomachs, or a thrilling vibration that we might have imagined. This was very,

very real. And it was growing. Soon, a roaring noise sliced through the caves, growling louder and louder, rumbling toward us. I couldn't move. I looked at Shona. Her lips were moving—but I couldn't hear a thing. The rumble turned into a high-pitched whine, shrieking and screaming through the hole into the tunnel. I slammed my hands over my ears.

The next thing I knew, Shona had grabbed one of my hands. She pulled it away from my head. "We have to get OUT OF HERE!" she was yelling in my ear. "QUICK!"

I'd forgotten how to move. My tail, my arms, everything had turned completely stiff.

"Come *on!*" Shona yanked my arm, pulling me with her. My body jackknifed into action and we hammered through the tunnel as an explosion erupted in the water behind us.

I turned around to see the end of the tunnel crumble and dissolve. Rocks fell and bounced in the water, scattering sand and bubbles everywhere, clouds bunching and spilling across the seabed like lava.

Something was reaching out from the tunnel, feeling around. Oh, God! What *was* it? A huge tube, slimy and dark green, almost as thick as the tunnel itself. One side was rubbery and shiny, then it flipped and twisted over and its underside was gray and covered in black spots. They looked like giant warts. In between them, great thick suckers grabbed onto the wall like the suction cups on the soap holder Mom keeps in the shower, only about fifty times bigger—and a hundred times uglier.

That was it! That was what I saw in my mind only moments ago—and now it was here, for real, in front of me!

The tube flapped and flicked about, maniacally batting and thwacking against the sides, reaching out farther and farther toward us. An icy stake of terror pinned me to the spot.

The siren noise shrieked into the cave again as the tube thing moved around in the tunnel, feeling its way along. Getting closer!

Someone was screaming and screaming.

Shona shook me. "Emily, you have to pull yourself together!" she yelled. The screaming stopped. It had been me. She pulled me through the water. "Just swim for your life!"

We threw ourselves along the tunnel, working our arms like windmills in a tornado. I tore brief glances behind us as we swam. The tube lashed out, extending toward us like a giant worm, ripping at the tunnel walls and doubling my panic.

Propelling myself faster than I had ever swum in my life, I flung my body through the passage until I finally made it to the open space. The rock was collapsing around us as we swam.

The thing was reaching out of the tunnel toward us! No! Its end was tapered and blood red, and covered with brown hairy strands swirling around as it felt its way through the tunnel. It slid farther and farther out as we dashed across the cave to the next tunnel, the one that would get us out of here.

CRASH! THWACK! Slamming against the roof of the cave, the walls, the ground, the monster worm was destroying the cave, little by little. We were almost within its reach. *Swim! Swim! Faster!*

As we heaved ourselves into the next tunnel, I glanced behind me again. The giant worm wasn't on its own. There were at least three others, maybe more, all searching and feeling around the cave walls, crashing through the water, reaching out toward us. Slimy, scaly tentacles. What *was* it? A giant octopus?

A scream burned silently in my throat. Shona had virtually disappeared. She was ahead of me, but the water was murky with swirling pieces of rock and debris. *One more corner, one more corner,* I repeated to myself again and again as I plowed down the long narrow tunnel.

I threw myself at the end of the tunnel. Nearly out! I was panting and gasping, my energy slipping away. And then a tentacle spun out, coiling itself down the tunnel. It touched me! *Arrggghhh!* Rubbery slime grazed my arm. My speed instantly tripled.

A moment later, I was out. Out of the tunnel! Back outside in the channel between the cliffs. Sunlight.

Shona was there, panting and heaving.

"It touched me! It touched me!" I screeched.

"Keep moving," she said.

But I looked back. And this time I saw something I hadn't noticed before.

"Shona!"

"I told you, keep—"

"Look." I pointed at the wall. How had I not seen it before? Carved into the wall. A trident. Neptune's trident! The huge pitchfork he carries everywhere with him. Instantly, an image flashed into my mind: the last time I'd seen Neptune. Standing in front of him in his courtroom, his booming voice issuing orders that no one would ever dare to disobey, the trident held out—the instrument that could create an island or a storm with a single movement.

"Keep moving," Shona said again. But her face had turned white.

We swam on, scattering shoals of tiny yellow fish as we pounded through the creek. Back into the lagoon, and out through the hole on the other side. Turning to close the curtain of reeds, I noticed the wooden plaques again. They were covered in algae, but there was something underneath. I rubbed at the algae, brushed reeds away — and I could see it. Another trident. We'd been trespassing in Neptune's own territory!

What had we done?

Shona was ahead of me. I caught up to her without speaking. Swimming in silence, I could hardly believe any of this had really happened. Everything was totally still and quiet. No movement at all. We stopped, listened.

"It didn't follow us," I said lamely. "We're safe. It's OK."

Shona looked at me. There was something in her expression that I'd never seen before. A hardness in her eyes. "You think, Emily?" she said. "You really think so?"

Then she turned and swam on. She didn't say another word all the way back.

My whole reason for coming to the lagoon, to secure Shona's friendship and my place on the island—all my hopes, and I'd done completely the opposite. I had no words either.

Well, I don't know about you, but this is not MY idea of a luxury cruise!

Swimming pool? I don't *think* so. Nonstop food and drink? Uh, hello? Enormous ship? Yeah, right!

We've been conned. Our vacation of a lifetime, full of "magic" and "enchantment," turns out to be two weeks on an old wreck of a sailing boat with me, Mom, Dad, and some old guy to drive us. Fabulous.

There's absolutely zilch to do. We've been out at sea for—well, I think it might be two days, but it's hard to tell since there's nothing to distinguish one deadly boring second from the next. I'll never forgive my parents for this. Especially Dad. Why did he have to see that stupid magazine?

And guess who's left to entertain herself all day while her parents go back to being totally wrapped up in themselves?

He's the only one who's enjoying himself. Mom's spent all her time inside so far, cooking or sleeping and occasionally turning green and rushing over to the side to be sick. Why I thought it might be different I don't know. When will I learn that nothing nice *ever* happens to me?

I wish one day it would. Just once.

Even the captain looks like death warmed over most of the time. Just stands at the wheel looking out at the sea. Not that there's anything else to look at. He hardly talks to any of us. He must be at least fifty, so it's not as if I want to talk to him. But he could make a little effort.

Dad doesn't seem to realize that the rest of us are having the most awful vacation in the world. I wish he'd pay some attention to Mom, but he's too busy running around with a fishing net, getting all excited about the stupidest things. Like now, for example. I'm lying on the deck reading a magazine— well, trying to read. It's not exactly easy while you're careening up and down and having to watch out for water splashing all over the place. Dad's on the deck next to me, leaning over the edge with a pair of binoculars. He's wearing bright yellow shorts, and his back is bright red to complement them.

Then he leaps up. "Mandy, love. Come and see. Quickly!"

I put my magazine down. Maybe he's spotted the cruise that we're really supposed to be on. Perhaps this was just a joke and we're on our way to start our real vacation on a real ship! I look out to sea. "There's nothing there, Dad."

"Wait. He'll do it again soon."

Turns out he's seen a turtle. A turtle! Well, excuse me, but BIG DEAL!

I decide to go inside. It might be even duller in there, but at least Mom won't try to convince me that I'm having the time of my life.

Only something stops me. I squeeze past the captain, and I'm about to open the cabin door when I catch a glimpse of something. Not just a stupid turtle. A . . . well . . . a kind of nothingness. Just ahead of us, it's all dark. The sea looks black and shiny, and the sky above it is suddenly filled with heavy clouds. Great. That's all we need now, a thunderstorm.

I look at the captain. He's taken off his cap. He rubs his eyes.

"What is it?" I join him at the wheel.

"Look!" He's pointing to a load of dials. They've got numbers on them, but they're changing too fast to make any sense.

"What do they mean?"

He bends down to study the dials more closely. "They should stay pretty much constant," he says. "Might just be a loose connection."

"What about that?" I nod toward the compass. The pointer's spinning around like mad.

The captain wipes his cap across his forehead. Beads of sweat bubble down his face. "I don't know what's going on," he says, his voice quivering. "It happened once before. It's—we need to get away from here!"

The boat's heading toward the darkness. And I don't know why I haven't thought of this before now, but I suddenly remember a comprehension test we did in English, about the Bermuda Triangle. It was called "The Ocean's Graveyard," and it was about all these ships that sailed into the Bermuda Triangle never to return.

The Bermuda Triangle. Is that where we are?

I glance across at Dad on the back deck. He's still staring through his binoculars.

"Dad."

"Hang on, I think there might be another one in a sec."

"Dad!"

He puts his binoculars down. "What?"

I point ahead, at the darkness. We're getting closer and closer. It's as though we're being pulled along, toward where the water's lying motionless and black.

Dad turns around. "Mother of . . . what's that?"

We gaze in paralyzed silence as the boat slowly begins to pick up speed, gliding toward the glassy blackness.

I don't notice Mom coming out from below deck, but at some point I'm aware that she's there, too. We're slipping over to one side as we career through the water.

"We're going to drown," Mom says suddenly. Almost calmly.

"Not if I can help it!" The captain grabs at the wheel, flinging it around as hard as he can. But it hardly makes any difference. His cheeks are purple. "Hold on!" he yells.

We're edging closer toward the silent black water. It's pulling us sideways, drawing us in like a magnet. We're slipping farther and farther to the side. Bits of spray spatter the deck. The boat starts to rock.

Mom's fallen onto her knees. The captain's lurching at the wheel. I'm gripping the mast. I reach out to Mom. "Get hold of my hand!" Spray lashes against my face as the boat leans farther and farther over to the side. Mom reaches out, our fingertips almost touching before she slips back across the deck.

"Maureen!" Dad lets go of the rail to reach out for Mom. He's holding her in one arm, gripping the rail with his other hand. He's got his arm around her—at last. I didn't want it to happen like this.

The captain is shouting something at us. He's spinning the wheel one way, then another. It's not making the slightest bit of difference. I can't hear what he's saying. I think I'm shouting, too. I don't even know what *I'm* saying. Seawater is everywhere. We're spinning sideways toward the strange glassiness, mast first, the bottom of the ship almost out of the water.

All is darkness, water, shouting, screaming. We're going to die! Out here in the middle of nowhere, on our own. A stupid, stupid death. I close my eyes and wait for the boat to veer into the blackness.

And it does.

Or it starts to.

We're teetering on our side when the boat suddenly jiggles and shakes. It's leveling out. What's happening? It slips and rocks a bit, there's water all over the deck and I'm soaking, but we're straightening out. We're not going to die! We're safe! Everything's going to be—

But then I see Dad's face, gray and heavy, as though he's suddenly aged thirty years. He's staring at something behind me.

"Don't tell me you've seen another turtle," I say shakily.

Then the boat lurches again and I fall to the floor. That's when I see it, rising out of the water. *What is it?*

First, huge tusks, curving upward like giant bayonets. Below them, a long, long, olive-green lumpy snout. It's taller than the ship's mast. It almost blocks out the sun. Horror seeps into my body. Huge white eyes bulging and popping out like great big fat full moons on either side, lumps all over the snout. Oh, GOD!

Enormous tentacles slap the water, extending outward and up, khaki-green greasy things with suckers all the way down, waving around, splashing, making a whirlpool. We're spinning into it.

I'm trying to scream, but all I can manage is a kind of dry clicking sound. We're being sucked into something, into the whirlpool, a mass of tentacles rising all around us.

And then Mom's screaming. I think maybe I am, too. One of the tentacles reaches right up into the air, then hurls itself down toward the boat and grips the mast.

I'm screaming for Mom; the boat's on its side. Where's Dad?

Water everywhere, a crashing sound, and then—

Chapter Four

S hona didn't talk to me all week—that first week in our new home. It was supposed to be a fresh start, a dream come true. Instead it was the worst week of my life. Think Brightport Junior High's worst moments and multiply by a hundred. I was still the odd one out, still the one who didn't fit in, who no one wanted to know. Was it always going to be like this for me?

Shona started hanging around with Marina and Althea. Maybe she thought anyone was better than me. Maybe she was right. After all, I was the idiot who had finally gotten to live with both of my parents and been given a new life on an island full of merpeople and glistening turquoise sea and white sandy beaches, and what did I do? I couldn't bear to think about it.

And yet I couldn't think of anything else. I even forgot to be scared of starting school. I drifted through it, like everything else, in a daze. I couldn't even get excited when I learned to dive with the grace of a dolphin and brush my hair like a real mermaid and sing the wordless songs of the sirens. None of it mattered. Everything was ruined because of what I'd done, and marred by a constant fear of the consequences. What was going to happen? Had it already started? The weather had changed a little since we went in the cave. Nothing all that dramatic. It had just been really windy, sudden sharp gusts making the sea all choppy. Probably just coincidence, but people had been commenting on it.

Millie and Archie came over one night. Millie stared at me all the way through dinner. "Are you all right?" she asked as she helped herself to a huge scoop of ice cream.

Mom turned to look at me, cupping my chin in her hand. "Are you, sweetie?" she asked softly. "You have been quiet."

"I'm fine!" I snapped. "Why shouldn't I be?"

"Your aura's looking gray and patchy," Millie said. "Usually means you're fighting demons in your mind."

Dad burst out laughing. "Don't think my little 'un would stand a chance against demons," he said with a smile. Millie glared at him.

I got up to clear some plates. Anything to get away. But just then, the boat rocked violently as a wave thrashed against the side, knocking half the dishes from the table and tipping me back into my seat.

Archie and Dad darted outside to see what had happened while I helped Mom and Millie pick up the broken dishes.

"Freak wave," Archie said, pulling his hair behind his head as they swam back up to the trapdoor to join us again. "Seem to have been a few of those lately. Wonder what that's about. I'll have to report back to Neptune about this."

"Neptune? Why?" I asked.

"It's my job to keep him informed of everything. That a problem?" He seemed to look at me suspiciously as he spoke. I must have imagined it. A freak wave couldn't have anything to do with me—could it?

On Friday morning, I bumped into Shona on the way to school. She'd avoided me all week but could hardly pretend she hadn't seen me when I was right beside her in the water. For a brief second, I wondered if she wanted to make friends again, but the look on her face said otherwise. Her expression was like mine when I'm faced with a plate of mushy peas, or a spider near my bed.

"Have you told anyone?" she asked, pulling me into a tiny cavern that led off from the main tunnel toward Emerald Cave.

"No! I don't know what to say. What are we going to do?"

"WE?" She stared at me. *"I* didn't even want to go up that stupid creek in the first place! *I* didn't want to go in the cave. *I* didn't want to knock the wall down. *I* am not going to do *anything!"*

A tear burned the corner of my eye. I'd never seen Shona like this. "Well, what am *I* going to do, then?"

"I don't think we should say anything," she said more softly. "We just forget it, OK?"

"Forget it?"

"Pretend it didn't happen. Whatever it was, it must have gone back where it came from. It didn't follow us. So we say nothing. Please?"

"But what if—"

"Em, think about it. We've only just gotten

here. Do you want everyone to hate us before we've even had the chance to make any friends?"

"Of course not. But—"

"But nothing. We leave it. Please, Emily."

I nodded. "OK." A drop of water plopped down from the ceiling into the pool between us. "You're still my best friend, aren't you?" I asked as we set off along the tunnel.

Shona didn't meet my eyes. "Let's just act normal, OK?"

A couple of merboys were coming along the tunnel. Shona smiled at them as they caught up with us, and then swam ahead with them. I trailed behind, pretending to get something out of my bag. I didn't want anyone to think I was all on my own with no friends. Which is exactly what I was.

We hadn't gotten much farther when I noticed that the water around me was swaying and swirling. It was building up, spinning around. I tried to move forward but got thwacked against the side. The monster! Was it here?

The caves were shaking. A thin stalactite fell and crashed down from the ceiling, missing me by inches. I jerked backward through the water, scraping my back on the rock. Within seconds, merpeople were rushing from the caves.

"Quick—out!" a merboy shouted as he raced past me.

I didn't need telling twice. We pelted out through the tunnels, back to open water. Outside, others were already gathered. Someone was swimming in between them, talking to groups of people, telling them to move on. Then he turned and I saw his face. Archie!

What was going on?

I swam over to him. He hardly looked up. "Just follow the others," he said gravely. "We'll meet in the Grand Caves."

The Grand Caves? The ones Marina had told us about? But weren't they only for really special events?

I followed the others in a daze, my mind swirling with images of what I'd seen—and fears of the destruction and horror that might be ahead; thoughts churning like the sea.

I gasped as I entered the Grand Caves. Impossible shapes hung all around us: upside-down forests, frozen bunches of arrows waiting to fall as one, long paper-thin flaps that looked like dinosaur wings. Drips from the ceiling bounced off majestic boulders and into the pool, ringing out like church bells.

Ahead of me, a stone platform jutted over the water. On one side, thick, marblelike columns reached down from the ceiling into the depths of the water, frilly edges folding around them like icing on a cake. On the other, the wall stretched up like a cliff side, stalagmites lining its surface, clumped together in chunky groups. Lanterns glowed among them, spreading shimmering lights across the pool as they shook. The walls were still trembling. Surely it wasn't safe to be inside if there was an earthquake?

I looked around for someone I knew. Shona had disappeared. *Probably with Althea and Marina,* I thought miserably.

In front of me, a long wooden walkway divided the clear azure pool. A few people were carefully picking their way along it. I looked away, feeling guilty as I did so. The last thing I needed now was for Shona and the other mermaids to see me as one of the humans. They'd *never* want to be my friend then.

But then I spotted Mom! She was here, too, edging across the walkway with Millie.

"Mom!" I couldn't stop myself from shouting out. She looked up and waved briefly before grabbing the rails as the caves shook again. She pointed up to the stone benches that stretched high up on the cave's sides. I wondered if I should get out of the pool and join her. A glance at the mermaids. No. I was staying in the water. Then another mighty crash thundered through the caves, throwing me under, leaving me with no choice anyway.

Gasping, I gave myself up to the water. It wasn't as bad underwater: it was a little like a Jacuzzi. It might almost have been enjoyable if it wasn't for the fact that I didn't have a clue what was going on, my best friend wasn't speaking to me, and the island seemed to be crumbling around us.

As I resurfaced, I spotted Shona with Althea and Marina. I knew it! A shot of anger speared through me. It wasn't fair! I hadn't exactly gone to that lagoon on my own. She'd done wrong just as much as I had. Nearly. I mean, it wasn't as if I'd forced her to go. And it was their suggestion in the first place! She looked up and caught my eye, just for a second. I nearly smiled. Then Althea said something to her and she turned away. She didn't look back. Traitor.

This was worse than Brightport Junior High! At least then, I could sneak out at night to meet Shona. Now I'd lost her, and it seemed as if all three of them had turned against me. It was so unfair! I'd be better off going back to Brightport, I thought, my heart heavy, my eyes stinging with tears.

I didn't have long to dwell on it. All thoughts were catapulted out of my mind by an explosion of rocks as the caves shook even more violently. A column that looked like marble fell into the water with a mighty splash. Forests of stalagmites shuddered and trembled. I looked up to see Mom gripping the bench. Millie was holding her arm and looking serene. As serene as anyone can look when they're sitting on a bench that seems to be doubling as a seaside rodeo horse.

Where was Dad? I scanned the pools. And then I saw him. Terror on his face, he was hurtling across the pool.

"Emily!" he cried into my hair as he pulled me toward him.

I grabbed onto him while the caves crashed and crumbled all around us. It was growing louder. It sounded like thunder, cracking right over our heads, coming from everywhere.

And then something happened. Something almost familiar. I almost knew it was going to happen, almost remembered it from somewhere else.

The shaking stopped.

Just like that.

The sudden stillness was almost as much of a

shock as the violent movement that had come before it, throwing people across the floor, dunking merfolk under the water. I gripped Dad so hard it must have hurt him. He held me close.

"Look!" Someone was calling out. I turned to see where everyone was looking. The caves were splitting! A crack opened up, starting from the base, shaking and creaking as it crumbled open. The whole thing would fall in on us. We'd be buried alive! Oh, God. The monster—the monster! It was here! I fought back waves of terror.

But I soon realized that nothing else was moving. Just one section of the caves was splitting open, almost like a hidden door. Almost as though it was being opened by someone. Or something.

Or Neptune.

The caves had split wide and high enough to let in a thick shaft of sunlight. I had to cover my eyes.

When I opened them, I saw him, riding into the caves, shrouded by dusty sunbeams. First the dolphins, then the chariot, gold and grand, carrying Neptune into the caves.

I should have known I'd be found out! His voice burst into my memory so clearly I could almost hear it. The memory so sharp: standing in front of him in his courtroom listening to him tell us we'd be spared prison on the condition

we'd come to this island. "If you break this condition, you will be punished most severely," he'd
added in that booming voice of his. Had I broken
it? What would he do to me?

The dolphins pulled Neptune into the center
of the caves before swimming back into the corners, surrounding us like bodyguards. Archie swam
beside the chariot.

Pausing to wait for silence, Neptune rose in
his seat, lifting his trident in the air. As he waved
it above his head, the cave closed again, sealing us
together to face his wrath. I knew what *that* was
like. Knowing I was to face it again was almost
enough to make me give up hope altogether.

Neptune looked around the caves. "Do you
KNOW why I am here?" he asked, his voice deep
and grave. His sentence echoed over and over,
*KNOW why I am here, KNOW why I, KNOW,
know . . .*

No one dared to answer. No one knew.
Almost no one. He was here for me — I was sure
of it. I tried to calm my thumping chest before
Dad heard it.

"I shall ask another question," he said, his voice
ringing around the caves. "Do you know why
YOU are here?"

He looked around, narrowing his eyes. I willed

myself to shrink into nothingness. Luckily his gaze passed me by.

More silence. Neptune clicked his fingers. At once, a line of sea horses appeared at the side of the caves. They gathered into a perfect formation and swam toward him. Then, hooking his golden gown in their tails, they raised it up behind him. Neptune sat down and nodded curtly, his diamond-studded tail fanning out in front of him. The sea horses instantly darted away.

"I will tell you," Neptune said. "You are here because of ME! Because of MY generosity. This island hasn't always been the happy little paradise you have here today. This was once a place of grave importance."

He banged his trident on a rock. "Archieval!"

Archie swam forward. Then, bowing low, he kissed Neptune's tail. "Your Majesty," he said solemnly. I'd never seen Archie look like this. He had a gold sash running along his tail; his hair was tied back in a neat ponytail and seemed to shine with splashes of deep green against the pool's reflection.

"Tell these folk their history," Neptune said coldly. "It's about time they were reminded." Then he sat back in his chariot, waving his trident at Archie to beckon him forward.

The caves became silent as we waited for Archie to speak.

He cleared his throat. "Many years ago," he began, "life here was very different. The Bermuda Triangle was an important stronghold. Together with a most trusty servant of Neptune's, our bravest sirens worked well here, in the rich waters around Allpoints Island." Archie paused. His tail flicked nervously. His cheeks had reddened a touch. "This is where ships were brought down. They were relieved of their riches, which were returned to the rightful owner of all that passes on the oceans."

Ships were brought down? That wasn't what he'd told us on the way here. He'd just said that they'd disappeared, not that they were brought down on purpose! Right here! Was our new home one of those ships? Maybe someone had died in my bedroom!

My mind swirled with grim and gruesome images: bodies under my bed, killed by the "trusty servant." Did he mean the monster? This place wasn't paradise at all. It was more like a setting for a horror film. I could hardly concentrate as Neptune started talking again. "Thank you, Archieval. And then what happened?"

Archie glanced back at Neptune before clearing his throat again. "The, er, the trusty servant I told you about. One day, he—"

"TELL THEM WHEN!" Neptune exploded.

"Almost a hundred years ago—"

"EXACTLY! NOT a hundred! Ninety-two years ago! Do you hear me? Ninety-two. That is my POINT!" As he shouted, a wave washed through the pool. I held on to Dad to steady myself.

Neptune sat back down in his chariot, his face purple with rage. He clicked his fingers and a dolphin rushed forward. Turning onto its back, it flapped its tail in front of Neptune's face like a fan. After a while, Neptune cooled down and he waved the dolphin away. He motioned to Archie once again. "Continue."

"Ninety-two years ago, this trusty servant went to sleep."

Dad pulled away from me. "You're talking in riddles, Archie."

What was he doing? Had he forgotten how powerful Neptune was? Or that it was only thanks to him that we were here? Or how easy it would be for Neptune to send him back to *prison*? He let go of me and swam toward Archie. "Tell us what this is about. Who is the trusty servant that you keep mentioning? If you're telling us a story, tell us the whole thing."

Archie glanced at Neptune, who shrugged disdainfully.

"All right," Archie said. "I'll tell you." He took a deep breath. "I'm talking about the kraken."

The cave filled with sound: people whispering, talking, gasping. Merpeople turning to each other with questions on their faces and fear in their eyes.

A mergirl from my class was in front of me in the water. "What's the kraken?" I asked in a whisper. I think in my heart I already knew.

"It's a huge, fierce monster," she whispered back. "It's just a myth, though. It's not real." She turned back to face Archie. "Or at least that's what we've always thought."

My body shook. My tail was spinning so vigorously the water was frothing around me.

A mermaid I didn't recognize held up her hand. She had deep wrinkles in her face and piercing blue eyes. "Archieval, if this is true, why didn't our parents tell us about it? My great-grandparents would have been alive while it was around. Surely they would have passed this on."

Archie glanced once more at Neptune for approval. A brief nod in reply.

"The merfolk who lived here at that time were the kraken's keepers. The kraken works for a hundred years, then sleeps for another hundred. The last time it went to sleep, one small ship somehow managed to find its way through the Triangle's border. With no kraken to bring it down, the ship ended up here." Archie looked at the people sitting along the stone benches. "Those folk were your ancestors," he said.

"But we don't know anything about this," one of the women called down. I recognized her from one of the ships in our bay. "Surely someone would have told us!"

"Once the people had landed on the island, it turned out that many of the merfolk were happy for them to stay. In a short time, friendships were formed. Apart from a very small number of the kraken keepers who were assigned to special duties elsewhere, most of the merfolk decided to stay here, as did most of the humans."

"You haven't answered my question!" the woman shouted.

"Memory drug," Archie said simply. "They volunteered. That was their choice."

"All of them?" the woman insisted. "The merfolk, too?"

"We can use it on anyone," Archie replied. "And it will wipe out almost everything. What remains—well, you have all heard half-tales, stories you never quite knew what to make of, myths passed on and distorted with every telling."

Archie's words were slowly filtering into my brain. I didn't want to understand, didn't dare to follow his thinking to its logical conclusion. But the memory drug, well, I knew all about that. It was what my mom had been given for twelve years, so she wouldn't remember that she was married to a merman. Fed to her in so-called treats from her so-called friend Mr. Beeston, the so-called lighthouse keeper! He'd always given me the creeps. He used to drop by to visit Mom all the time, for coffee and doughnuts. He never said a lot, but he just had this really odd manner. He'd look at me sideways, and his eyes were different colors and his teeth were crooked. Well, he just made me feel uncomfortable. And then, when it turned out he'd been spying on us my entire life, it all made sense.

I'd half forgiven him in the end, when he helped me get back at Mandy Rushton. He used the memory drug on my class so no one would remember me turning into a mermaid. But he wasn't to be trusted—and neither was anyone else who went around doling out that drug!

"As you all know, Neptune is a just and kind ruler," Archie continued with a slight cough. "He allowed them to live together here on the island.

No one needed to know about the kraken. Not yet. And so, you are here today. Allpoints Island has existed in this way for ninety-two years."

A mermaid with glitter in her hair and a pink tail that flicked and splashed on the water raised her hand. "But why are you telling us this?" she asked in a timid voice. "Why now? And who are you, anyway? We hardly know you."

Neptune rose from his chariot, motioning Archie to move out of his way. "Archieval works for me," he said. "And he has told you your history. Now let me tell you something about your present."

He sucked in his cheeks, clenching his teeth. "Someone," he said, almost in a whisper, "*someone* has dared to challenge my power." He took a breath, lifting his trident in the air. Then, in a voice that shook the caves as much as his arrival had, he bellowed, "Someone woke the kraken before its time!"

Darting backward and forward in the pool, agitated and angry, he spoke quickly. "Eight more years. That's how long it had. That's how long it NEEDED. That's when I would have been here for it. But no! Someone couldn't wait that long. SOMEONE had to wake it early. Do you KNOW what happens when my kraken has not had the sleep it needs?"

The caves responded with silence. No one was going to attempt to answer Neptune in this kind of mood. Not that he was known for having any other kind of mood.

"I'll tell you. It wakes in a rage. Too much of a rage for even NEPTUNE to calm it. My truly loyal servant—someone has robbed me of it!"

"What will it do?" someone asked.

"The first signs are relatively small. It will lash around in its lair, creating freak waves. This is what it does while it is still in its cave. As far as we know, it still IS in there. But it will find its way to open seas sooner or later, and when it does, it will set out on the only path it knows." Neptune paused as he slowly surveyed the caves. "Destruction."

My tail was shaking again. "It's OK, little 'un," Dad whispered, pulling me close. "I'll look after you." He knew nothing. Nothing.

"That is why I am the ONLY one who should wake the kraken. The one who wakes it is the ONLY one who—" Neptune stopped abruptly. He smoothed back his hair and straightened his beard.

"Well. Let me just tell you this. Without my direction, it can destroy anything in its wake. Perhaps this whole island will crumble from its rage."

The end of the island? All because of me?

I tried to swallow and found I couldn't. I had to fix this!

"Oh yes," Neptune continued. "And you should know this: it can bring ships toward it. Apart from a few of my loyal aides, the kraken is the only creature who knows how to pierce the magic of the Bermuda Triangle. Once the kraken leaves its cave, you are no longer safe. Discovery cannot be far away. When this happens, the days of Allpoints Island are numbered."

Neptune sucked in his breath again. "I have not yet decided what I shall do about you all. In the meantime, I want to know WHO DID THIS! I WILL find out! It is IMPERATIVE that he or she come to me!"

He stared around the caves in the silence. An occasional drop of water plopped softly into the water. No! I couldn't. I *couldn't*! I *wasn't* going to get Mom and Dad thrown off the island. I wasn't going back to that awful jail. I had to think of something.

"WELL?" he bellowed.

Then someone coughed gently. There was a bustling sound up on the stone benches. Someone was getting up. Millie! What on earth was she doing?

She flung her black cape over her shoulder

and stepped toward a barrier at the edge of the pool.

"Your Majesty," she said firmly. "I'm not one to interfere, but I may be able to help you."

Neptune almost smiled. He looked as though he was smiling, anyway. It might just as easily have been anger twisting his face into a contorted frown. He pulled on his beard. "*Help* me?" he repeated.

"I can see things," Millie explained. "I don't like to boast, but I *have* been told I have something of a gift. I just need your star sign."

"My STAR SIGN?" Neptune yelled.

"Yes, you know, your horoscope, your—"

"I know what you mean! It's PISCES, of course!"

"Thank you," Millie said through tight lips. "That anger won't do your karma any good at all," she added in a stage whisper. Then she closed her eyes and folded her hands over her chest. "I believe I can tell you exactly what has happened," she said. "I just need some quiet."

Neptune looked as though he was about to burst, but he didn't speak. Nor did anyone else. Could she really see what had happened? Millie's cosmic ways didn't often come to much, but she did have an accurate moment now and then. What if this was one of them?

"I see riches of some sort," Millie murmured. "What is it? Gold? Let me focus."

Gold! She was describing the cave! No! Trust Millie to have one of her flukes and get it right when I desperately needed her to come out with her usual wacky nonsense. I'd heard enough. I had to get out before she told them everything. Maybe her vision had me in it!

I glanced up and tried to catch Mom's eye. She was watching Millie with a look of admiration on her face. How would she look at me when she found out what I'd done? I couldn't bear to imagine it.

I edged quietly away from Dad toward the darkness at the back of the pool. I could hear Millie's voice warbling across the water. She sounded as if she was humming. Everyone was watching her. This was my only chance.

"I'm sorry," I whispered into the darkness, and slipped quietly away.

I swam frantically through the dark tunnels, not even thinking about where they were leading me. I pounded past underwater stalagmites faintly lit up with soft, glowing crystals, around twists and turns and crevasses, almost gasping for the sight of the sky. I had to get out of the caves. Had to think.

Eventually, I came out into the open water. The light shocked me. Two little blueheads hovered at the cave's mouth, pecking at the rock as though giving it little kisses.

A noise behind me. Splashing. Someone was following me!

I dived down into a thin cave under the rocks, stumbling upon a group of fat hogfish who looked up at me with black eyes before scattering away to find another den.

I watched the cave's entrance. It was Dad!

I swam out from under the rock. "What are you doing here?"

"Emily!" He swam over toward me. "Why have you run away?"

I retreated farther under the rocks. "I've let you down. You, Mom, everyone. We'll get thrown off the island and it's all my fault. I'm so sorry."

Dad squeezed into the crevasse with me, scattering clouds of sand as he slithered along the rock. "No one's going to throw you off the island, little 'un. Why would they do that?"

"You don't know!" I wailed. "You don't know what I've done." A tear snaked down my cheek, mingling with the water. All this time! All those years without him, and now that I'd found him,

I'd done something so stupid, so awful, he'd hate me forever. I'd ruined everything.

"What? What have you done?"

I bit hard on my lip, squeezing my eyes shut.

"Whatever it is, you can tell me. We'll figure out what to do together."

My face was wet with tears. "It was me!" I blurted out. "*I* woke the kraken!"

"You *what*? But how——"

"I went exploring! I knew I shouldn't have, but I did. It was in a cave. I'm so stupid! I found it. I woke it up, Dad. I've ruined everything. I'll never be able to show my face on the island again. You've only just got out of prison and now——oh, Dad, I'm sorry."

Dad stroked my face. "Look. I don't quite understand, but it'll be OK. We'll fix this. I'll look after you."

I pushed his hand away. "Dad, it *won't* be OK. Don't lie to me. I'm not a *baby*!"

He stared at me, his face red as though I'd hit him. As I held his gaze, he nodded slowly, as though he was watching me grow up in front of his eyes, catching up with who I really was, instead of who he remembered me being. "You're right," he said eventually. "Of course you're not." He turned to swim away.

"Wait." I grabbed his arm. "I'm sorry."

"You know what you are?" he asked, his voice as tight as his mouth.

I shook my head, holding back fresh tears.

"You're my daughter, that's what you are. You're a Windsnap. And you know what that means?" Before I had a chance to answer, he added, "It means we're going to straighten this out."

"I'm not going back to the meeting. I can't. Please."

"Who said anything about going back there?"

"What, then?"

Dad stopped swimming and searched my face. "We're going to the cave. Show me where it happened."

"The *kraken's* cave?"

"Why not? You heard what Neptune said. It's probably still in there. Maybe we can straighten this mess out, somehow. Seal it back up so it's safe again or something."

"Dad, it was really frightening. It was the most terrifying thing ever!"

"Worse than going back to face Neptune? You stood up to him in his own court, remember."

I dropped my head. "I know. That was pretty frightening, too."

"Exactly. And you did that, so you can handle this as well."

"I suppose."

"Come on." He held out his hand. "Let's see what we can do."

Letting out a breath it felt as if I'd been holding in for a week, I took his hand and we swam on.

"It's that way," I said as we came to the lagoon. It looked different. The water was murky and muddier than I remembered. Sand-colored flat-fish skimmed over the seabed, moving beneath us like shifting ground.

My throat closed up. We'd reached the carving on the wall. The trident. How on earth could we have missed it last time? Maybe if we'd seen it, none of this would have happened.

It was pointless thinking like that.

We came to the pinwheel, except this time when I looked at it, I realized I knew exactly what it was. The long shoots spiraling out from the round body in the center . . .

"That's it," I said, my voice rippling like a breaking wave. "I don't want to go any farther."

He stopped swimming. "We need to do this, little 'un—I mean, Emily."

"Dad, you know, it's OK if you want to call me—"

"No." He put a finger over my lips. In charge. Strong. "You're not a baby. You're a scale off the old tail, and I couldn't be more proud of you. And we're going to get to the bottom of this, find out what we can, right?"

"But it's out of bounds. This was how the whole trouble started."

"And this is how it'll end, too," he said. "You don't think we found ourselves at this place by the pair of us doing what we were told, do you?"

I didn't say anything.

He reached out for my hand. "Come on. I'll go ahead, but you need to tell me where I'm going. I'll look after you."

Eventually, I took his hand and we swam in silence.

Everything looked familiar, until we came to an enormous gash in the rock. Maybe the size of a house.

"In there." I held out a shaky arm. "Except it was a tiny hole last time!"

Dad swallowed. "OK, then. You ready?"

"I'll never be ready to go back in there." A solitary fish flashed past me: soft green on one side, bright blue on the other, its see-through fins stretched back as it swam away from the cave. Sensible fish.

"Come on. You'll be OK. I'm right beside you." He squeezed my hand and we edged inside, slipping back through the rock.

But it was completely different. So different that I started to wonder if we were in the wrong place. There were no thin winding channels, just huge gaping chasms all the way. We swam through them all.

And then we came to the gold. We *were* in the right place. Jewels and crystals lay scattered across the seabed. As we swam lower, the surroundings felt less familiar. Colder. And there was something else. Something very different. The deeper we got, the more we saw of them.

Bones.

Just a few at first, that could perhaps have passed for driftwood. Then more: clumps of them, piled up like the remains of a huge banquet. Long thin bones, twisty fat ones—and then a skull, lying on the sea floor. A dark fish slipped through an eye socket. I clapped a hand across my mouth.

"Dad!" I gripped his hand so hard I felt his knuckles crack.

"Don't look at them," he said, his voice wobbling. "Just stay close to me."

We swam into every bit of the cave. Every inch.

"What do you see?" Dad asked as we paused in the center of the biggest chasm.

I looked around. "Nothing."

"Exactly." He turned to face me, suddenly not in charge anymore. Not strong. Just scared. "It's gone, Emily. The kraken—it's on the loose."

How long have we been here? A couple of days?
Who knows? All I know is we're stranded on a
deserted scrap of an island, the boat's broken, and
I'm hungry.

And scared.

Nuts! How long can a person live on nuts? And
water from an iffy-looking stream. Dad figures he'll
catch us some fish. And he thinks we could fix the
boat if we all "shaped up a little." He's acting as if
he's on some kind of Boy Scout trip, as if this is all
part of the adventure. I know he's putting it on,
though. It's too manic. I can see the truth in his
eyes. He's just as scared as I am.

Mom's hardly spoken. It's best that way. If we
talked more, we might end up talking about what happened. About how we could have died. About the . . .

Anyway.

It's hardly even an island. I can vaguely see
something that might be a real island, out at sea.

Far too far to swim. Just our luck to get stranded on this tiny speck of land instead. Two hundred paces from one side to the other. I counted yesterday. Or the day before, I don't remember. Some time when I was collecting twigs so that Dad could build us a so-called shelter. Not that I'm likely to get any sleep. It lends itself to a touch of insomnia, getting stranded on an island the size of a pair of underpants, with nothing to eat, no way of getting home, and no one to talk to except your parents.

Not even the captain.

That's another thing we don't talk about. I try not to think about that, either. What happened to him? Could he be—

My hands start to shake uncontrollably. My legs feel as if they'll give way any second now. Like I said, best not to think about that.

There's a splashing noise behind me.

"Mandy! Where's your mom?" It's Dad, coming out of the water with one of the nets from the boat. He's wearing purple shorts down to his knees and he's waddling onto shore in his flippers. He's been off looking for fish. That's all he's done since we've been here. That and mess around banging and hammering on the boat. It's washed up on the tiny beach, half-filled with water and littered with shells and stones and broken bottles. Yeah, sure, Dad. It's going to be so easy to fix.

The net's empty, as usual.

Dad pulls his mask and snorkel off. He's grinning. What on earth can he find to smile about? Doesn't he realize we're stranded and we're all going to die? Maybe he got knocked on the head when the boat went under.

He's shaking himself dry. "Come with me. I've got something important to tell you both."

I follow him back to the pathetic bundle of twigs that seems to have become our home. Mom's sitting on the ground leaning against a palm tree. She's not doing anything, just staring into space. Her hair's sticking out everywhere, as though she's had an electric shock. Her face is white, her eyes unfocused. She looks like a madwoman.

"Maureen, Mandy—our problems are over!" Dad announces.

I can't help it; I burst out laughing. I mean, look around you, Dad—wake up and smell the coffee. Oh, sorry, I forgot. THERE ISN'T ANY COFFEE BECAUSE WE'RE MAROONED ON A STRIP OF LAND YOU COULD MISS IF YOU BLINKED, WITH NOTHING BUT NUTS, INSECTS, AND A SMASHED-UP BOAT FOR COMPANY!

"Just hear me out," Dad says. "You're not going to believe me, but I swear, every word is true." There's a tic beating against his red cheek. "I *swear*," he repeats.

Mom sighs. "Just tell us. What ridiculous idea have you come up with now?"

"It's not an idea, Mo. Well, not exactly. It's something I've seen."

Mom raises her head a fraction. "What have you seen, then?"

Dad puffs out his chest and looks from one of us to the other. "Mermaids." I watch the lump in his throat bob up and down. "I've seen mermaids."

"Oh, for heaven's sake, Jack!" Mom pulls herself up and shakes out her skirt. "When are you going to act like a proper man and fix this mess, rather than indulging your stupid fantasies?"

She starts to walk off, wiping sand off the backs of her legs. Dad grabs her arm. "It is not a fantasy, Maureen!" he says furiously. "I swear on every breath I've ever taken, there are mermaids! Not here, farther out. I've seen them swimming, under the water. They've got tails—long, glistening, shiny tails!"

Their eyes are locked. It's as if they're acting out some surreal sketch and the teacher has just said "OK, freeze, everybody!"

But there's something about what he's said; something just out of reach . . .

"Don't you understand what this means?" Dad says. His neck's bright red and bulging. He's gripping Mom's arm.

Mom stares at him. "No, Jack. I'm afraid I don't

know what it means at all. That you're cracking up, perhaps? Well—don't worry, I'm sure I won't be far behind you." She pulls out of his grip.

"Mo, I'm *not* cracking up!" he shouts. "You've got to believe me! We could save our home, the amusement arcade—the whole pier!" He turns to me, his eyes wild and intense. "Mandy, you believe me, don't you?"

"I—" Of course I don't believe him. Of *course* I don't! But there's something. Something. What is it?

Mom's shaking her head. "You'll forgive me if I don't quite follow your logic."

Dad holds up his net. "We capture one! Take it back to Brightport. We can have it on show, charge admission and everything. We'll take care of it, of course. Give it a good life. People will travel from all over the country to see it! From all over the world, maybe! We'll be heroes in the town; we'll pay for the pier to be renovated. Don't you see? This could solve all our problems!"

Mom sucks in her cheeks. "Jack," she says, "you haven't managed to catch so much as a *goldfish* since we got here! Even if I were to believe that you have seen a mermaid—which, frankly, I don't—how in heaven do you propose to catch the thing?"

Dad pulls at his net. "I haven't got the whole plan figured out yet, have I? I've only just *seen* them. A group of them. Swimming in the deep water. One of them had gold stars shining in her tail. There was a merman too, with long black hair and a shiny silver tail. A merman! For God's sake, Maureen!" He grips her arm again. "I'm telling the truth! You'll see I am."

Mom pulls away and turns to me. "Come on, Mandy. Help me get some dinner. I've had enough of your father and his daydreams for one afternoon."

I follow Mom as we pick our way through undergrowth, scavenging for food like vagrants. As usual, we don't talk. But this time, it's because of the thoughts going around in my head, thoughts I'm not sure I dare share with Mom. There's definitely something familiar about what Dad said. Something niggling away in the back of my mind. I can't put my finger on it.

Maybe it's something I've seen on TV. A film about mermaids or something. I've got this picture in my mind. Someone swimming. She's got a tail and she's spinning around, smiling, grinning—at me! She's in a pool. It's not from TV. I'm sure it isn't. It feels real. It feels like a memory.

I grab a couple of nuts and shove them hard into my pocket. Mermaids! As if! I force myself to laugh.

We'd better get away from here before we *all* crack up.

Chapter Five

D ad."

He didn't reply. Just kept on staring out to sea. We'd spent half the day swimming around the coast, trying to keep out of sight, and trying to figure out what to do next. We stopped to rest at a large rocky bay on the east side of the island, just a little farther down from our bay.

I swam over to join him next to a huge boulder at the edge of the bay. "Dad," I said again.

"I'm thinking," he said without turning around. "Just give me a minute."

I counted to ten. "What are we going to do?"

He shook his head. "I don't know, Em. I just don't know."

I looked out to sea with him. The water lapped gently into the cove behind us. Daylight was starting to fade.

I stared out at the horizon. So much ocean, stretching for miles and miles and miles—forever, it seemed. Nothing but water. And the monster. Somewhere. A cold shiver rattled through my body. The water lay still, but how long till it would seethe with the kraken's rage? The stillness was almost worse—knowing it was out there, waiting.

Something flickered on the horizon. A brief flash of light. I jerked upright and peered so hard my eyes watered. There it was again.

"Dad!"

"Emily, will you leave me alone! I've told you, give me five minutes. I need to think."

I shook his arm. "Look!" I pointed out to the horizon.

Dad followed the line of my finger. "Mothering mussels," he breathed, squinting into the distance. His words came out like a whistle. "What's that doing there?"

"What is it?"

"Look—red, then green." Dad turned to me. "It's a ship, Emily."

A ship had gotten in! The kraken had already pierced the Triangle's border.

"It's not coming any closer, is it?" I asked with a gulp. What if it was? One way or another, that would spell disaster. Either the kraken would destroy the ship—or the ship would discover us. Either way, it was completely unthinkable.

"Doesn't look like it. Doesn't mean it won't, though." Dad pushed off from the rock and started to swim away. "Come on."

"Where are we going?"

"We'll have to say something."

"Say something?" My words jammed up my throat. I swallowed hard. "Who to?"

"I don't know. Archie, I guess." Dad took hold of my hand. "Emily, there's a ship coming toward the island. The others need to know that the kraken's gotten out."

"No! Dad, they'll want to know everything. They'll make you tell them it was all my fault."

"Em, love, the monster could attack that ship. Or the ship could discover us here. That'll be the end of us all. You heard what Neptune said. We can't stay here if the secret gets out. Can't you just see it? Hordes of tourists swarming the place? They'll turn us into a zoo or something." He turned to swim away.

A zoo. My old fears of discovery resurfaced in a wave of anguish. That was one of the nightmares I used to have in Brightport. What had I *done*?

"There must be something we can do," I said, swimming hard to keep up.

"This is the only thing." Dad's voice was firm.

He didn't speak again. The water soon grew warmer as we reached the shallow sand, rippling like tire tracks across the sea floor.

Dad wouldn't look at me. "You go along home. Mom'll be worried."

"What about you?"

"I'm going to see if I can find Archie."

I didn't move.

"It'll be all right," he said with a tight smile. Then he turned and swam toward the end of the bay, taking my last shreds of hope with him.

Mom threw her arms around me the second I arrived back at *Fortuna*. "Emily! I've been worried sick. Where've you been?"

"With Dad. I felt claustrophobic in the caves and we—we went exploring." My cheeks burned. I hate lying to Mom.

"Mary P., you really should listen to me. I told you she was safe," Millie said, pouring some herbal tea from a pot and settling down on the big sofa.

"Millie saw a ship," Mom said.

"She *saw* it?" I burst out.

Mom looked at me quizzically. "When she did Neptune's reading. She had a vision of a ship. What ship did you think I meant?"

"Oh. No. Nothing. Yes, that's what I thought you meant," I blustered. *Great move, Emily. Just give the game away to* everyone. "I thought you'd said something about gold." I tried to keep my voice even.

"Yes, well, you can't be expected to get everything right, all the time," Millie replied, sniffing as she picked up a magazine.

"So what did Neptune say about the vision?" I asked, holding my breath.

Millie flipped the pages. "Not everyone appreciates my gift."

"He told her he'd throw her off the island if she wasted any more of his time with her hocus-pocus," said Mom, smiling.

How could she smile? I could hardly *speak*. I had to get away from here. "I'm going to my room," I said. Before they had a chance to argue, I'd gone through to the back of the ship and closed my door behind me. Shaking, I sat down on my bed and looked around. Like all the others, the room had a trapdoor that led to the floor below, to the sea. I'd hardly used it yet. The one in the living room was open all the time and it was bigger.

I crept over to the trapdoor next to my bed and opened it. Maybe . . .

"Emily." Mom was at my door.

I jumped away from the trapdoor. "I was just looking at the fish," I said quickly.

"Are you all right?" Mom stepped into the room and came over to me. She lifted a strand of hair off my face, stroking it behind my ear. "If there's anything you want to talk about . . ."

"There isn't," I said, trying to make myself smile. I imagine I looked like a scared rabbit with a twitch. A while ago, I could talk to Mom about anything, and didn't know how to relate to Dad at all. Funny how things had changed. If *funny* was the right word. Which it wasn't.

"I'm fine, honestly," I said. "Just a little tired." I stretched my mouth into a yawn. "Look, see. I think I'll have a nap."

Mom stared at me quizzically for a moment before shrugging. "Well, we'll be next door if you need anything." She kissed my forehead and left.

I waited five minutes. She didn't come back. OK, this was it. I knew what I was going to do.

I had to get to the ship, make it change its course or something—just stop it from causing disaster to everyone on board, and probably all of us on the island too. I didn't have a clue how I was going to do it; I just knew I had to try.

I eased myself through the hole. Then, dangling over the side, I lowered myself down as gently as I could and let go. I dropped with a splash. Had they heard? I held my breath and waited. Nothing.

I waited a little longer, to make sure my tail had fully formed. When the tingling and numbness had completely gone, I ducked under, swam through the big open porthole, and headed toward the ship.

It was almost like the old days: swimming out to sea under a sky gradually filling up with stars. A striped butterfly fish raced along beside me before slipping away into the darkness and disappearing under a rock. Shoals of silver bar jacks hovered nearby, shining like pins in the darkness. Purple fans waved with the current, caressing me as I sailed over them.

It was nothing like the old days.

In the old days, I was swimming out to meet my best friend; now I didn't even know if I still *had* one. Shona would have been by my side on an adventure like this. My chest hurt as I pushed myself to swim harder, swim away from the painful thoughts. The water grew colder and darker. I picked my way out toward the ship, praying there was no current around this side of the island.

After a while, I stopped to scan the horizon. Two dim lights, facing me. It was a long way out, but definitely inside the Triangle. I couldn't even see the island anymore. Just blackness, except— what was that? Something flashed through the water. A boat? I held my breath while I watched. Nothing. It must have just been the moon's reflection.

I swam on toward the ship. I had to stop it from finding us, get it away from the island. I had to buy some time.

Eventually, I was close enough to study it: a cruise liner with three levels of portholes and balconies, all lit up with lamps. The sides rose steeply out of the water.

I swam all around it, looking for a way in. There was a rope ladder hanging down at the back. I tried to make a grab for it but missed by inches. I heaved and jumped up in the water. No good—it was just out of reach.

I swam around again, looking for something else. And right at the front, I found it. The anchor!

Gripping the chains, I pulled myself out of

the water. My tail dangled and flapped in the sea. Panting and gritting my teeth, I managed to inch my way up. Eventually, I'd done it. I clung onto the chain like a koala, my body clear of the water. Within moments, I got that tingly sensation I knew so well. My legs had come back.

I hooked my feet into the loops, then slowly and carefully climbed up to the ship's deck.

Hauling myself over the metal rail, I landed heavily on the deck. A quick look around. No one. Just me and the darkness and a row of deck chairs. I dried myself on a towel someone had left on one of them and pulled on the shorts I'd brought with me. Then I went to look for some signs of life.

It didn't take long.

Halfway down the side of the ship, I found some stairs and a door that led inside. There were sounds, somewhere near. I followed the noise, almost sniffing my way toward it. Music. Laughter.

Soon I came out of the narrow corridor into an open space with a few people dotted around. I tried to saunter in casually, as though I belonged there, even though I knew I'd be spotted in a second.

But I wasn't. Some kids were playing in a tiny

arcade on one side; on the other, a couple of men were drinking at a small bar. A man and woman behind the bar laughed together. No one even looked up.

A flight of stairs led up toward where the real noise was coming from. *OK, you can do it.* I took a deep breath, twirled my hair a few times, nibbled on my thumbnails—and went upstairs.

It wasn't till I saw all the food that I realized I was starving! I'd hardly eaten all day.

I grabbed a paper plate and joined the line behind a girl who looked about my age. Maybe she'd know something.

"It's great, this vacation, isn't it?" I said as we shuffled along the food table, shoving tiny sausages and crackers and chips onto our plates.

"Mm," the girl replied through a pizza slice.

"Wonder how long before we shove off," I said casually.

She swallowed her bite of pizza. "My mom says we're not even supposed to be here. She thinks we've gone off course. Doesn't matter though, if we see it."

See it?

"Yeah, that's what I thought," I said, trying to stay calm. I popped a mini sausage into my mouth. "So has anyone seen it yet?"

The girl put her plate down. "Don't you know?"

"Oh, I, um—I forget. Remind me?"

"That's why we're here! Mom says more than half the passengers canceled at the last minute. That's how we got our places. I bet Carefree Cruises is totally fed up with that captain!"

What was she going on about?

"Yeah, I bet," I said seriously. "What did he do again?" I asked, quickly turning away to grab another handful of chips.

"How can you not know? He saw Triggy, of course! First sighting in absolutely YEARS!"

A chip got stuck halfway down my throat. "Triggy?" I asked, swallowing hard.

"Don't tell me you haven't heard of Triggy."

I tried a lighthearted shrug and a frown.

"Triggy! The Triangle Monster! I've always believed in it. Mom said it was just a silly fairy tale, but now she's not so sure. I hope we see it, don't you?"

I couldn't reply. I couldn't do anything. I tried. I opened my mouth, even moved my lips a little, I think. But nothing came out. *Triggy?* It sounded like a cartoon character. She had no idea! I thought of the slimy tentacles racing down the tunnel toward me, the suckers all along it, grabbing at the walls, the way it extended out, the hairy tapered end touching me.

The bones.

Now these people were hunting it down. Which either meant it wouldn't be long before they found us — or they'd be its next victims.

"I — I've got to go now," I said eventually. I staggered away from the food table.

"See you in the morning," she called before going back to the table.

"Yeah." *Whatever.*

I stumbled back down the stairs. At the bottom, I took a turn that I thought led back to the corridor I'd come down earlier. But I emerged into another open space. I was about to turn back when I noticed a shop just ahead of me. It was closed now, but there was a poster in the window. I went over to take a closer look.

It was the front page of a newspaper: the *Newlando Times.*

BRAVE CAPTAIN TELLS OF HORROR AT SEA the headline screamed across the top of the page. I read on.

The old myth of Triggy the Triangle Monster rose up again today when Captain Jimmy Olsthwaite was rescued from stormy seas by a local fisherman.

Captain Olsthwaite lost his boat when it was attacked by what he described as "a monster beyond imagining. The size of a dinosaur! And a dozen tentacles that wrapped around the boat."

His story has horrified and delighted tourists in equal measure.

Katie Hartnett was among those setting sail today with Carefree Cruises. "It's so exciting," she told the *Newlando Times.* "My parents used to tell me stories about the Triangle Monster when I was little— but we never thought it might exist for real!"

Others have canceled in droves. Retiree Harold Winters was among them. "We wanted a peaceful trip, not the fright of our lives," he said.

The captain's sighting has not been confirmed. The coast guard is warning that it could be a case of delirium brought on by his traumatic capsize and rescue.

Three others were believed to be onboard

the boat with the captain. Neither they nor the boat have yet been recovered.

The boat was owned by a company called Mermaid Tours.

I stumbled away from the shop. I was in one of those nightmares where you're stuck somewhere, trying every exit, but there's no way out and every step takes you deeper into the horror. It had happened already. The monster had attacked a ship, all because of me. My head swirled with nausea and panic.

I found myself out on the deck again. I leaned over the railing, and my stomach heaved. My mouth tasted like iron. I looked down at the sea, deep navy in the darkness. Little bright flecks sparkled white as the water lapped and splashed against the ship. There was another boat down there. I could just make out its shape. A small yacht. It looked as if it was coming toward us. Maybe they were checking to see if their lifeboats were working or something. Well, they'd be needing them soon, unless I could come up with a miracle.

I had to do something! I couldn't just stand here staring at the sea.

Then it came to me.

I ran up steps, down ladders, along corridors,

banged on doors, called through open windows: "TRIGGY! THE MONSTER!"

People emerged from their rooms. Dressing gowns were pulled around bare bellies and boxer shorts; women came out of their cabins in silk nighties, kids in twisted-up pajamas.

"Triggy!" I shouted at everyone I saw. "The monster! I've seen it!"

"Where?" Open-mouthed gasps.

"Over there!" I pointed—away from the island. I pointed and pointed. "Tell everyone. Tell the crew!" I ran on as everyone I spoke to gathered along one side of the boat: all gazing out to sea, desperate for a sighting of something I wished with all my heart I would never see again.

I had to find the captain.

I ran on, down more corridors—until I barged slap-bang into someone.

"Hey, what's all this?" It was a woman in a uniform. She grabbed hold of my elbows, holding me at arms' length.

"I need to find the captain," I gasped. "I've seen the monster!"

The woman frowned. "Yes, dear. I'm sure you have. Now, come on, why don't you—"

"I have!" I burst out. "I can prove it. It's— it's—" I gulped. The memory of it took the breath out of me for a second. I started again. "It's enormous, and it's got tentacles."

"We've all seen the papers, sweetheart," the woman said, smiling. "Now, if you want an excuse to visit the captain, you can just say so. He's always happy for you kids to have a quick look around the cabin."

Bingo! "OK!"

The woman gently shook her head as she pointed toward some stairs. "It's up there. Turn right at the top, straight on to the end, and it's through the door ahead of you. But knock first. He doesn't take kindly to being barged in on."

"Thanks!" I took the stairs three at a time.

I bashed on the door. *Come on, come on!*

No one answered. *Come* on*!* No time for politeness. I tried the door. It swung open.

"I need to talk to the captain," I said breathlessly as I burst into the room.

Two men were sitting in front of a load of dials drinking coffee. One of them swiveled around. "Now, hang on. What's the—"

"Are you the captain?"

"I certainly am," he said, "and you can't just—"

"I've seen the sea monster!"

The captain leaned forward in his seat. "The sea monster?"

I nodded.

His face relaxed into a slight smile. "Now, listen, you want me to tell you something about this sea monster?" he asked. I swallowed, and nodded again.

He lowered his voice. "It doesn't exist."

I held his eyes. "It does! I've seen it."

The captain leaned back in his seat. "OK, let's have it, then. Big thing with tentacles, was it?"

"Yes! That's exactly what it was!"

"Right." He was smiling, laughing at me. I had to convince him.

"It's—it's enormous!"

"Mm-hm. Anything else?" the captain asked in a bored voice.

"The tentacles—they're tapered at the end."

He turned back to his tea. I racked my brain. *What else—what else?*

"And hairy! And they've got huge great suckers all along them!" I blurted.

The captain put his cup down. "They what?" he asked, his face suddenly hard, and focused on mine.

"And they're—they're green, and gray underneath, and warty . . ." My voice trailed away as I remembered the sight of it. My teeth chattered.

The captain turned to the other man. "That's exactly what my friend at the coast guard said."

"Sir, the newspaper report—"

The captain shook his head. "Those things weren't in there. Come on, man. Face the facts. You saw the dials. You know we've been stuck here, spinning on the spot like a child's top."

"Yes, but you said yourself that if we made a mammoth effort, we could get out of it."

"Exactly, and we need to do that now. There's something going on and it's time we faced up to it."

He moved his chair closer to mine and leaned toward me. "OK, then," he said. "You'd better tell me exactly where you saw the sea monster...."

I'd done it! The ship had changed direction and we were heading directly away from the island.

I sneaked along the empty deck. Every single person on the ship must have been crowded on the other side, peering into the darkness for a sight of something they thought would make their vacation. I thought of its flailing tentacles, the floor littered with bones, and I shivered. If only they knew. I hoped for their sake that they never would.

I had to get back to the island. Maybe I could confess, after all. If I told Neptune what I'd done here, how I'd stopped a whole cruise ship full of people from discovering us, he might even for-give me.

I checked around one final time to make sure no one could see me. Then I slipped back into the water.

Moments later, the familiar warm feeling spread through my legs as they turned back into my tail. It shone bright in the moonlight.

Fish around me seemed to be dancing. I could make out their shapes in the darkness. They must have been happy for me. Maybe it was a sign. Everything was going to be all right. I swam along, lost in my hopes that I could somehow make up for everything that had happened over the last couple of weeks. Perhaps Shona and I would be best friends again and the island would be safe. The kraken might even go away and our lives in our new home could really start.

"EMILY!"

I started and looked back, twisting around in the water. Two people were leaning out over a balcony on the cruise ship, waving frantically. Why weren't they on the other side with everyone else? I edged back toward the boat.

That's when I saw who it was. Mom! Thin and wiry with wild hair, waving her arms. Someone was with her. Larger than life in a black cape. Millie! What the heck were—

"Emily!" Mom screamed again.

I swam closer to the ship, but it was picking up speed. I could hardly keep up.

"Watch the propellers!" Mom screeched. "Don't come too close!"

Millie had sunk into a deck chair next to her, her head in her hands. A small yacht was moored on a buoy, near where the ship had been only moments ago. The one I'd seen coming toward us. I recognized it now: it was our old boat! They'd followed me!

"Mom! What are you doing there?"

"We came to find you, but you'd just jumped off! It was Millie's idea. The vision, the boat. She'd seen you on it."

"What? You never told me that."

Millie got up and stumbled across to clutch onto the railing. "I kept it to myself," she wailed. "I thought it would have sounded crazy. I've heard what people say about me." She leaned out over the railing. "I'm sorry, Emily. I was too busy worrying about my reputation."

"We didn't think they'd get going again tonight." Mom called.

Oh no. My fault again. I'd made things worse *again*. The ship was only on the move because of me. And now it was moving faster and faster away—and taking my mom with it!

"Mom!" I tried to keep up. She was shouting something, but I couldn't hear her anymore. I could hardly even see her as the ship picked up speed.

"MOM!" I yelled again, uselessly, into the darkness.

As the ship slipped away, I let the current carry me along. No energy left. I drifted away from the ship, from the island, from everything that mattered. Tears streamed down my face as I howled in the darkness.

And then—

Noise.

Clattering—shuffling. What was happening? I mopped my cheeks with my palms.

I'd got caught in—what? Seaweed? I flapped and scratched at it. *Please, not the monster.* I looked around me.

A net! I was trapped in a net! A man was holding it, pulling at a piece of rope, dragging me through the water, propelling himself along with flippers.

Flapping my tail, I tried to push myself away, but he was too strong. I struggled and fought, biting at the net, pulling at it with my fingers, cutting my hands, scraping myself all over. It was like wire. There was no way I could get through it. I scratched and screamed as he drew me through the sea.

Soon the water grew warmer and shallower. We were at a tiny island: a little sandy bay with a few palm trees, a small boat moored to a pole, and a makeshift lantern propped on the beach. The man tied my net to the pole.

He pushed his mask and snorkel onto the top of his head. I couldn't make out his face properly in the shadowy light. "I'm not going to hurt you," he said, panting from swimming so hard. "Trust me."

I didn't say anything.

"Do—you—speak—English?" he asked in a very loud voice. I ignored him.

"Stay here," he said, as though I had a choice. He disappeared up the beach as I scraped and scratched at the net, trying to get out. Moments later, he was back with someone.

"Dad, you are completely obsessed," a girl's voice was saying. "It's the middle of the night!" The voice sounded familiar. But it couldn't be.

"I said, didn't I?" the man replied as they came closer. "I told you—I TOLD you! *Now* do you believe me?" He pointed in my direction. The other person waded toward me and peered at me in the darkness. As she came closer, I could just make out her face from the lantern's light.

It was—

It was—

I gasped and jerked backward against the net, my mouth stupidly open. It couldn't be! How—?

It was someone I knew. Someone I knew well. Someone I'd thought I would never *ever* have to see again.

Dad's caught a fish at last.

Hallelujah.

He's screaming and yelling at me to come and see it. You'd think no one had ever caught a fish in the sea before.

But it's not a fish. He's got someone with him.

"I told you! I told you!" he's yelling. "I said I'd catch a mermaid, didn't I? Do you believe me now?"

I get closer, and I notice a tail. No! It can't be!

He has! He's actually caught a mermaid!

It turns around. I see its face, its mousy hair, skinny little arms. It *can't* be! It's impossible! But it is. It is. I grab the lamp and bring it closer as I stare at her.

It's Emily Windsnap!

And then I remember. I remember everything! The pool, the swimming lessons. She came to us once before she left, showing off as usual. She had a tail! She swam in front of us all, swirling it around. Grinning at me as if to say she'd won. It wasn't enough for her that everyone thought she was *so* wonderful. Julia, the swimming instructor—they all liked her more than they liked me, all thought she was better than me. She had to rub it in, didn't she? Had to prove they were right. As if I didn't already know it.

How could I have forgotten?

There was something afterward—they gave us doughnuts. That was when it all faded. The doughnuts! Had they drugged us or something? And what the heck is she doing *here*?

Our eyes meet. She's as shocked as I am.

"Mandy!" she says.

I pull myself together quickly. "Oh, hi, Emily," I say, nice and calm. I sniff and turn to Dad. "Why are you bothering with *her,* Dad?"

Dad pulls off his mask and snorkel. "What are you talking about, Mandy? It's a mermaid!"

"Dad, have you actually looked at her face?"

He gawks at me for a second before turning to Emily and then back to me. I can almost see the realization crawling into his mind. He points at Emily. "But that's, that looks like—"

"Yeah, Dad," I say, trying to sound bored, or at least as if I've got a *clue* what's going on here, "it's Emily Windsnap."

"But how . . . but she's a . . ." His voice trails away. He looks at her again, then at me. "Don't be stupid, Mandy," he says suddenly. "Of course it's not Emily Windsnap. It just looks a little like her. This is a mermaid!"

Mom joins us on the beach. "What's the fuss, Jack?"

Dad runs toward her, ignoring me, and ignoring reality, it seems. "No time now, Maureen," he says. "We need to get ready. Where's all our stuff?"

"What stuff?"

"Everything. Everything we need. Get it in the boat. We're off as soon as it's light."

"Off?" I follow Dad out of the water. "What d'you mean 'off'? Where are we going?"

Dad stops and turns back to me. "We're going home, Mandy. With our mermaid. We're going to save the pier. Just like I said."

He runs over toward the boat.

"But it's broken!" I say, following after him. "We capsized, remember?"

"I've been working day and night on this boat," he calls back. "I think she's ready to sail again. Pack your things, and then get some more sleep. First light of dawn and we're off."

"Mom?"

Her eyes are vacant. She looks as if she's already given up hope. "I haven't got a clue what's going on," she says. "What's that he's got in the net?"

I leave her to find out for herself as I follow Dad

to the boat. Maybe we can sort everything out. Maybe he's right. It's worth a try, I suppose. Anything's better than rotting on this stupid island for the rest of our lives. Even if it does mean sailing home with *fish girl*.

The boat seems to be just about holding up. It would be better if Dad had the slightest idea how to sail it. We're buffeting about all over the place. He keeps staring at the navigation dials and then yelling things at Mom, like "Get over onto starboard!" and "We need to tack! Watch the boom! Hard alee!"

She yells things back, but her words are washed away by the wind and by the seawater spraying us on the back deck. Just as well. Judging by her expression, it's probably best if neither of us can hear what she's actually saying.

Anyway, I'm busy with Emily. I've got to keep an eye on the net, make sure it doesn't come loose. Can't have her escaping.

"Comfy down there, are you?" I call down to her. She's being pulled along like a water-skier. "Enjoying your little trip?"

"What are you going to do with me?" she whimpers. She's scared. I swallow my guilt. Why shouldn't she suffer? Why shouldn't she understand how *I* feel most of the time? Would it hurt for someone to understand?

"Oh, didn't Dad tell you? We're taking you back to Brightport," I say.

The boat swerves and surges, so I don't hear her reply. Just a kind of yelp from inside the net.

"Yeah, we're going to put you on display," I continue when she bobs above the surface again, her hair plastered across her face with seawater. I smile down at her. "Hey, maybe all your old school friends will come and visit. That'd be nice for you, wouldn't it? We were thinking maybe five dollars a visit. What d'you think?"

"What about my mom? She's stranded on a ship! I've got to find her! And my dad? Let me at least get a message to him!"

I want to. Part of me wants to shout and cry and ask why it has to be like this. But I can't. Show her my weakness and she can hurt me even more. Forget it.

"Yeah, right," I say.

"Mandy, I need you!" Dad's calling.

"Back soon," I call down to fish girl. "Don't go anywhere now. Oh, sorry, I forgot. You can't!"

I stand up to see what Dad wants. But I don't need to ask. The boat has leveled out; all is calm. But just ahead of us is something I'd almost forgotten about.

The darkness, spreading like an oil slick in the pale morning light, pulling us in.

"Dad, what are we going to do?"

He shakes his head. "I haven't got a clue, dear. We've got to get across it, somehow."

Mom's inching along the side deck to join us. "Jack, are you crazy? Have you forgotten what happened last time? The last two weeks foraging for food like beggars after nearly drowning? And that *poor* captain. *Have* you?"

"What choice do we have, Maureen?"

"We can think about our choices as soon as you've gotten us away from here. But I, for one, am not going to gamble with my life when the odds look like that!" She points to the sheet of water, glistening like glass ahead of us.

"Well, *I,* for one, am not going to live on nuts and berries for the rest of my life!" Dad yells. "And I'm not going to go back and watch my home and my livelihood demolished either."

"So you'll kill us all then, will you?" Mom screams.

"Mom! Dad!" I try to get between them, but the boat suddenly lurches and I slip across the deck. We're starting to tilt. We're being drawn toward it again. "Please—please don't fight."

Neither of them is listening. They'd rather scream at each other than try to work out what to do.

"DAD!" I yell, clutching the railing as the boat dips farther. I nearly fall over the side. Emily is down below in her stupid net. We're going to capsize again. I'm going to drown out here, all because of *her*. I can't believe it!

The boat lurches again.

"I can help." A voice from down below.

"What?"

"I'll help you."

I grab the railing as the boat leans over. Spray hits us on all sides as we skid through the water, soaking me. She looks up at me pitifully, her big brown eyes round and shiny. I can't bear it. I turn away. I bet she's only putting it on anyway. "And why would you do that?" I ask.

"I don't want you to die," she says.

"I'm supposed to believe that, am I?"

"I've got enough on my conscience," she calls up. "I don't need that as well. You can keep me in the net. Just let the rope out. I'll pull you away."

I glance over at Mom and Dad. They're not screaming at each other anymore. Mom's trying to make her way over to me. She's not even holding on to anything.

"Mom! Stay where you are!"

"Let the rope out!" Emily yells. "Do you want to be killed?"

I glance at the rope. It's looped around and around over a hook. "Don't try to do anything clever, all right?"

"Just do it!" she shouts. "It'll be too late in a second."

I lurch over to the back of the boat. One last glance at the water ahead of us, then I unhook the rope. "I'm warning you!" I shout as I throw it into the water.

The coil lands with a splash. Then nothing. Where's she gone? She's disappeared! I scan the surface of the water. Where is she? She must be in there somewhere.

I'm staring so hard at the water it looks like it's changing color, getting darker. It *is* changing color! There's a shape in there! A huge gray outline of something—something very, very big. Something we saw before and like idiots pretended to ourselves we hadn't.

Without warning, it bursts through the surface. A piercing, screaming siren sound screeches into the sky as an olive-green tentacle rises up, way up above us, then sheers downward to wrap itself over the top of the boat like an arch.

No!

"Mandy!" Emily's yelling. Where is she? Did she know it was here? Did she somehow make this happen? I know it's a crazy thought—but maybe, I mean, she had the rope. She was in the water; she hates me. She could have done it. Just as I was starting to trust her—that'll teach me.

The monster lifts the boat right out of the water, high up into the air. I can see the underside of its tentacle. It looks like a giant worm, extending and retracting, slithery and lumpy. Gasping and retching, I fall against the railing, clutching on for my life.

With an almighty crash, it drops us back down onto the water, and the surface explodes.

We're such fools! How could we let it happen *again*? *She's* done this to us. She's made it happen. She tricked us somehow.

The thing has tentacles all over us, sliming over the boat, roaming, searching for things to grab and latch on to. I'm slipping across the deck, water every-where. It sucks the boat down, throws it around, tosses us one way and then another.

Any second now, we'll all be in the water. Should I pray?

As if praying would help.

The only thing giving me courage as the boat is thrown over, as I clutch the railings, hold my breath, and grab the lifebelt, is one single thought:

I'll get you for this, fish girl. I will SO get you for this.

Chapter Six

otal stillness. Utter darkness.

What had happened? Where was I?

I rubbed my eyes, tried to move. I was still inside the net, trapped under a rock. Out of the darkness, a shape was coming toward me. It looked like a submarine, gliding along the very bottom of the sea, black on top, white underneath, large fins flapping below. As it came closer, it opened its jaw. Serrated lines of teeth, above and below: the sharpest bread knives.

A killer whale!

I grabbed the net, rubbing it hard on the edge of the rock, sawing and scraping frantically. My fingers bleeding and raw, I yanked and tugged at the net. *Come on, come on! Break!*

The string started to fray and tear. I was nearly out.

But then the water was swirling all around me, whisking up and around, faster and faster, like a whirlpool.

It was back.

The sea filled with giant tentacles, writhing and grasping and sucking. I crouched tight under the rock and prayed it wouldn't see me.

THWACK! The tenticles crashed against a rock, only a few feet away from me. It split and crumbled instantly. My tail flapped wildly; my teeth rattled so hard my jaw hurt.

CRASH! The tentacles came down again, scattering a spiraling shoal of barracuda before searching for their next target.

And then they found it. The whale! Jaws wide open, the whale thrashed, snapping its teeth at the monster. I crouched under my rock as the kraken moved closer, and for the first time, I saw its face. I clapped a hand over my mouth, swallowing back a scream.

Horned and full of snarling lumps, with huge white eyes on either side of its head, it opened its mouth to reveal teeth like shining daggers. Briefly opened wide, its teeth came crashing together, snapping shut, again and again, pulling and tearing at the whale. On and on it went, flinging the whale from one side to the other as tentacles and horns and teeth grabbed and tore at its skin.

Eventually, the thrashing slowed. The whirlpool stopped. The sea began to change color, blood seeping into the cracks around me. *Go away, go away,* I said silently, over and over, until, miraculously, the water became calm again, almost as though it had heard me.

In the darkness, I cried.

Mom.

I kept seeing her, reaching out to me from the ship, wild and screaming as she was taken farther and farther away. The image bit into me like wire. I curled into a ball and tried to push it away.

I had to find Mandy and her parents. There was no way of knowing where I was or how to get back. I knew it might be madness to search for them but, much as I hated to admit it, they were my only hope now.

I tore at the net till I'd made a hole big enough to squeeze through. Edging out of my hiding place, I forced myself not to think about what I'd just witnessed, although my twitching body made it hard to forget. I scanned the water. Nothing. It had gone.

Swimming away from the rocks, I searched desperately for something familiar. I soon came to a deep sandy stretch, rocks on either side. Around them, weeds floated and swayed, surrounding me like a thick curtain. I swam along the sandy channel until it came to a rocky reef, full of holes and ridges and gray peaks like castles and hills.

I fought the rising panic in my chest. This wasn't familiar at all. I was completely lost. A large, sullen gray fish drifted silently ahead of me, hovering like a hawk. Bright blue eyes bore down on me as I passed it.

"Who's that?"

A voice! A male voice.

"Come no farther!" The voice called out again. I stopped swimming.

"Who are you?" My words bubbled away from me.

Silence. Then, "You'll do as I say. I am armed. Do you understand?"

Armed?

"I—yes, I understand." Understand? Of course I didn't! I didn't understand any of this.

Out of the shadows, a thin, lanky figure swam toward me. A young merman, maybe in his twenties. He pulled some fishing line out from a packet on his back. "Hold your arms out."

"Who are you? Why should I—"

"Do as I say!" he bellowed, reaching for something at his side that looked like a knife. I thrust my arms out in front of me and watched while he tied my wrists together. "This way."

With that, he turned and swam, pulling me along behind him. All thoughts of my mom and the kraken and Mandy were dragged away by this—my second capture in one day. I let myself be pulled along. What choice did I have? No strength left to fight, this time.

The reef stretched and curved, a lunar landscape dotted with ornamental gardens. Deep brown plants lined rocky chasms. Round boulderlike chunks of coral clung to every surface; thick green spongy tubes waved and pointed threateningly as we passed over them. I glanced at the merman as we swam. He had a thin gray tail with silver rings pierced along one side. Wild blond hair waved over his shoulders; a chain made of bones hung around his neck.

We came to a cave with green and blue weeds hanging down from the top of its mouth in a curtain. Crystals were embedded in the rock all around the entrance.

"In here." He pushed me forward.

"Where are we?"

"You'll see."

Inside, the cave ballooned out into an enormous dome. Crystals, jewels, and gold lined the route. Mosaics filled with gems of every color swirled along the seabed: a round body, swirling arms . . .

"Where are we?" I gasped. "Who are you?"

"You'll find out soon enough," he replied. We'd reached a building. It looked like a castle, or a ruin of a castle. Half-collapsed turrets were filled with diamonds; crumbling walls held pale jewels in clusters around their base. A giant archway for a door, a marble pillar on either side. As we came closer, I could see something embossed onto each pillar. A golden sea horse.

I knew this archway! I'd seen it before, or another one very much like it, when I was taken to Neptune's courtroom. "This is one of Neptune's palaces, isn't it?" I asked, shuddering as I realized we were swimming over a mosaic shaped like a mass of tentacles.

The merman didn't reply.

Through the arch, a chandelier hung from a high ceiling, jangling with the water's rocking. That confirmed my fear. Neptune had found me.

We ducked low to swim through a smaller

arch, adorned, like the others, with elaborate jewels. A wooden door lay ahead. The merman paused to neaten his hair. Then he turned a shiny brass handle and nudged me inside.

We were in a small room. A stone desk embedded with shells took up half the space. Conches and oyster shells lay scattered on its surface. Next to it, an old merman turned as we came into the room. He had a scraggly beard and dark eyes that stared at me, holding me still.

"What's this you've found, Kyle?" the merman asked in a deep grumble. As he spoke, he stroked something lying very, very still by his side. It looked like a giant snake. Greeny yellow with purple teddy bear eyes, its gills slowly opening and closing as its mouth did the same, it swayed its head gently around to face me. A moray eel!

I opened and closed my mouth too, rigid with fear. Nothing came out.

"She was trespassing, sir," Kyle answered briskly.

"Untie her. She won't try leaving here in a hurry, if she has any sense." The old merman smiled at his pet. It leered back, stretching up almost as tall as him.

Kyle clenched his sharp jaw into a scowl as he pulled at the fishing line. I rubbed my wrists. "Tell us how you got here," he demanded.

"I don't know!" I said, tearing my eyes away from the eel. "I don't even know where I am. I had an accident, got lost, and you found me." Then, trying to control the quiver in my voice, I added, "Can I go home?"

"Home?" The old merman leaned toward me. The eel rolled its neck down into a spiral and closed its eyes. "And where would that be?"

I looked away from him. "Allpoints Island."

The two of them exchanged a look. What was it? Shock?

"Allpoints Island?" Kyle blurted out. "So you know about—"

"Kyle!" the old merman snapped. "I'll handle this."

"Of course. Sorry." Kyle drew back, bowing slightly.

Pausing briefly to pat the moray, the old merman swam toward me. "Now then," he said in a voice as slimy as the eel, "I don't believe we've been introduced. I'm Nathiel. And you are . . . ?"

"Why should I tell you who I am?" I said, my heart bashing against my chest. "Why won't you let me go? What are you going to do with me?"

Nathiel laughed and turned away. "Questions, questions. Where shall we start, Kyle?"

Kyle shuffled his tail, pulling on his necklace. "Um . . ."

Nathiel waved him away. "Very well, little girl. I'll tell you who we are. Seeing as you've been kind enough to drop in. We are your biggest fear . . . or your greatest protectors. Depending on how you view your situation at this moment."

"You're not my biggest fear," I said, my heart thumping. "My biggest fear is much worse than you!"

"Oh yes?" Nathiel swam back toward me, no trace of kindness or favor on his face. He twitched his head and the eel rose up, uncoiling itself to slither along behind him. I flinched as it stretched almost up to my face.

"Do you know how powerful we are?" Nathiel asked in a quiet, biting voice. I shook my head quickly, without taking my eyes off the eel. "We are Neptune's chosen ones, his elite force, the only ones he trusts with his most prized possession." Nathiel edged an inch closer to me, his cold eyes shining into mine. "We, little visitor, are the kraken keepers."

A million questions jammed into my mind. "The kraken keepers? But if you're—but it's—"

Nathiel laughed, a throaty sound that echoed around the room. The eel slowly stretched up. It was about three times taller than me. *Please don't open your mouth, please don't open your mouth,* I prayed silently as its jaw twitched.

With another click of Nathiel's fingers, the eel slithered to the back of the room, folding itself once more into a perfect coil.

"Now," Nathiel said, "that's my side of the introductions. I think it's time we heard a little more about you. You see, we know quite a bit about Allpoints Island, don't we, Kyle?"

Kyle swam forward. Copying Nathiel's sneer, he replied, "Neptune tells us everything."

"That's right. So, for example, he tells us about merfolk who break his laws." Nathiel swam farther forward. "Merfolk who go meddling in places they shouldn't," he added, edging closer still, his nostrils flaring. "Merfolk who WAKE his beloved KRAKEN!" he shouted.

"But, I—how did you know?" I cried. My body was shaking. Water frothed around my tail. I tried to make it lie still.

Kyle stared at Nathiel. "Yes. How did you?"

"I *didn't* know!" Nathiel replied. "Swam right into it, didn't she? Come on, Kyle. What do you get if you add the kraken on the loose, an island full of merfolk who know nothing about it, and a scared merchild clearly running away from trouble? It's a simple case of mathematics."

"So we've found her?" Kyle said.

"We've done good work." Nathiel patted Kyle's

arm. "Neptune will be very pleased with us. Very pleased indeed."

"Neptune? You're going to tell him?" My voice quivered.

"Of course! That is the whole point. Don't you realize the danger we are all in, you foolish girl?"

"But Neptune! He'll be furious with me."

"You think we give a fin about that?" Kyle snapped. "We need you. All of us. There's more than just yourself to consider."

"What do you mean? What use am I to you?"

Nathiel shook his head. "Kyle, I've had enough of this whining. I think it's time we got the boss in."

"The boss? Neptune? He's coming here?" I squeaked.

"Not Neptune, no. One of his most trusted aides." Nathiel picked up a conch. Turning away from me, he spoke softly into it. I couldn't hear what he said. I quickly scanned the room, looking for an escape. My eyes met the eel's. *Try it,* they seemed to say. I shivered back against the wall.

"He'll be along very shortly." Nathiel put the conch down and tidied some shells on his desk.

A moment later, the door opened. I squeezed my eyes shut in terror. Someone was swimming toward me. I bit my lip as hard as I could, forcing tears away.

"Well, what have we here, then?" a voice said. A creepy voice.

A very familiar voice.

My eyes snapped open to see a crooked smile, an odd pair of eyes: one green, one blue. A scruffy-looking merman who wasn't all he seemed. Here he was again, all the way from Brightport.

It couldn't be! The so-called lighthouse keeper. Mom's so-called friend who was anything but that in reality.

"Hello, Emily," said Mr. Beeston.

He turned to the others. "Good work, both of you," he said, snapping something around my wrists. Handcuffs made from lobster's legs! They bit and scratched at me.

Then he pushed me toward the door. "I'll take over now," he said before turning back to give me another of his lopsided smiles. "It's time we were reacquainted."

How could they let this happen? Twice! I can't *believe* my parents! My dad. It's all his fault. I can't believe I agreed to this nightmare vacation in the first place.

We're hanging on to our useless, broken boat, lying across it, gripping onto ropes. Only problem is, it's upside down! How long before it sinks and we *totally* end our vacation in style? I grab the rope tighter as the swells carry us up and down. My stomach seesaws with them.

Are we through that, that whatever it was, that great big sheet of glass in the middle of the ocean?

And the other thing.

I refuse to think about it. It didn't happen. Mom and Dad haven't mentioned it. I must have imagined it. Delirious, that's what I am. It was probably just the waves. Or a vision, because I'd seen it before. Yes. That's it. Definitely. A mirage.

There's nothing to worry about. I'm just crack-ing up.

"Maureen, Mandy—look!" Dad lets go of the rope with one hand and points out to sea.

It's a ship. Coming toward us!

"Wave! Both of you! Splash your feet!" Dad yells. For the first time in our lives, Mom and I do what he says without arguing.

The ship's coming closer and closer. Have they seen us? They *must* have! There's nothing except us moving for miles all around. We're kicking and yelling, every atom of hope screaming out of us.

"I can't splash anymore, Dad. My legs are killing me." I stop kicking for a moment while I catch my breath. The ship's stopped moving. They haven't seen us, after all. That's it. There's nothing we can do now. The realization slams into my mind like a block of ice: we're going to die.

But then I notice something attached to the ship. "Look!"

They're lowering a lifeboat into the water! It's coming to get us.

We've been saved!

Chapter Seven

Mr. Beeston unhooked the lobster claws from my wrists and pulled out a couple of jelly-like cushions. He motioned for me to sit down on one of them while settling himself on the other. I'd hardly ever seen him as a merman. He was half-human and half-merperson like me, the only other one I'd met. He looked just as creepy either way, with his crooked teeth and his crooked smile and the odd-colored eyes that stared at you from the corners.

We were in a bubble-shaped room. It felt like the inside of a huge round shell. No windows, just one small hole divided by thick metal bars. Tiny chinks of light threw pencil-thin beams across the darkness. A black damselfish with fluorescent purple spots and a bright yellow tail weaved between the rays.

I tried to stay calm. My mind wouldn't stop racing, though. What were they going to do with me? Would anyone find me? Dad? Shona? Were they looking for me? And what about Mom and Millie? My heart ached at the thought of them on that ship. They'd be miles away by now.

"What are you doing here?" I asked in a daze. Among the millions of questions racing around in my head, it was the only one I could seem to form into words.

"Surprised to see me?" he asked, his voice slipping across the room like slime.

"Of course I'm surprised to see you! Who's taking care of the lighthouse in Brightport?"

"The lighthouse?" Mr. Beeston laughed. "Emily, why would I be taking care of a lighthouse?"

"It's what you do!"

"The lighthouse was a cover. You know that."

"Oh, yes. Of course," I said numbly. I'd found out before we left Brightport that Mr. Beeston was one of Neptune's agents and that he'd been spying on us to make sure we never found out about Dad. Well, it didn't work, did it? I found my dad. I'd beaten Mr. Beeston once. Maybe I could do it again. "But that still doesn't explain—"

"I was promoted," Mr. Beeston said, a crooked grin twitching at the side of his mouth. "For my bravery and good work."

"*Good work?*" I spluttered. "Is that what you call turning me and Mom over to Neptune? You were supposed to be our friend. We could have been thrown in prison, like my dad." I squeezed my eyes shut and pressed my fingernails tightly into my palms. I wasn't going to cry. He wasn't having that satisfaction.

Mr. Beeston flicked his tail nervously. "I— well, Emily, I did my duty. And look, I was needed here. They're working on rebuilding this palace, and there's a lot to do, monitoring activity in the area and keeping a gill open for any kraken-related incidents." He narrowed his eyes at me accusingly.

"So what are you going to do with me?"

"Do with you? It's not about what I want to do with you. It's about what you need to do for us."

"What d'you mean?"

Mr. Beeston shuffled forward in his cushion. I shuffled backward in mine. He tightened his lips. "I am still an agent of Neptune's, you know," he said sharply. "One of the highest ranking of all, now. And if I tell you that you are going to do something, you will do it. You don't question my authority."

I folded my arms, anxiously flicking my tail while I waited for him to continue.

"We are all in grave danger. The kraken is on the loose. It has to be calmed and brought back to Neptune."

"But what's that got to do with me?"

He held my eyes for a long time before replying.

"You, Emily, are the only one who can do it."

Someone was banging on the outside of the shell. Mr. Beeston opened the porthole-shaped door we'd come through. Kyle surged into the room on a sudden wave. It flung me against the wall.

"Sir," he said breathlessly. "I've had a sighting. It's coming closer. The sea—it's getting rough."

"Thank you, Kyle. Good work," Mr. Beeston said.

"It's heading toward the palace!" Kyle panted. "I think it's going to get us all. We might have to make our escape."

"Make our escape? Are you off your fins, boy?" Mr. Beeston barked. "Have you been given the wrong job? You have one purpose and one purpose only. You have a wonderful opportunity to return to the old days and restore the power of the kraken. Do you hear me?"

"Yes, sir." Kyle reddened. "I'm sorry."

"Now, don't let it out of your sight. I'm dealing with it. Have some faith."

Kyle retreated, leaving a swirling cloud of silt behind him.

"Are you going to explain any of this to me?" I asked as Mr. Beeston swam back into the room. A tiny silver fish swam toward him, slithering across his stomach. He batted it away.

"The kraken is Neptune's pet," Mr. Beeston began.

"I know that."

"And it sleeps for a hundred years. Without its full sleep, it wakes in a murderous rage."

"I know that too."

"Stop interrupting me, child! I shall tell you the story my way or not at all."

I slammed my mouth shut.

"All but Neptune are forbidden to approach the kraken during its sleep. Neptune is the only one who should wake it. And only at the specified time. You see, when it wakes, the only person it will listen to is the one who wakes it, the one it sees first on opening its eyes. This should always be Neptune. But this time, it was you."

"You mean . . . ?"

"Yes, Emily. The kraken will obey you and only you."

I realized I wasn't saying anything. My mouth moved. Opened. Closed. Nothing. The kraken would obey me and only me? I slumped back against the wall, my mind empty, my limbs numb. A thin ray of sunlight threw a diagonal line across the room like a dusty laser beam, lighting up barnacles that lined the walls. The beam shimmered and broke, rocked by the constant water movement.

"What do you want me to do?" I asked eventually.

"We need to move quickly. Neptune's power over the kraken is fiercely protected. It wasn't expected that anyone else would ever wake it. *Most* merfolk obey his rules." He paused to scowl briefly at me. "First, you have to go to the edge of the Triangle, where its magic is strongest."

"The edge of the Triangle?" I gasped. "You mean the current that leads to the deepest depths of the ocean?"

"Nonsense!" Mr. Beeston snapped. "It doesn't do that. That's what we tell folks to keep them out of the way."

"So where does it go, then?"

"It leads into the realm of the kraken."

"The realm of the kraken?" My voice cracked. Somehow, that didn't sound much more inviting than the deepest depths of the ocean.

"The place where you can communicate with it. You must go to the edge of the Triangle and come face to face with it."

"Face to face?" I burst out. "With the kraken?" I couldn't face the monster again. Please no! An image squirmed into my mind: those horrific tentacles, searching, batting and thrashing, smashing into the tunnel. My eyes began to sting with tears. I didn't care anymore if Mr. Beeston saw me cry. I couldn't hold it back.

He spoke softly. "It's the only way."

"What happens then?" I asked, swallowing hard. "When we're at the Triangle's edge?"

"It will come to you. It will listen to you."

"And I can save the day?"

"What? Yes, yes, of course you can save the day."

"And it'll do what I tell it?"

"As I told you, it will listen only to you. Its power lies in your hands."

I suddenly realized what Mr. Beeston was telling me. I could end all of this. I could bring the kraken into my power. It would listen to me. I could calm it down and everything would be all right. I just had to face it one more time.

"OK," I said. "I'll do it."

Mr. Beeston smiled his crooked smile. "I knew you would."

He turned to leave. "There's just one last thing," he said, pausing at the door. "You *were* on your own when you woke the kraken, weren't you?"

"I — why do you want to know that?" I blustered.

Mr. Beeston darted back toward me. Coming so close that I could see the jagged points of his crooked yellow teeth, he leaned into my face. "If someone else was with you when the kraken woke, we need them too."

"Why?" I asked in a tiny voice.

"Emily, if there was someone else there, it means the kraken will not obey you on your own. Whoever it saw on waking, that is who it will obey — whether that is one person or twenty. We need them all or the plan will fail."

"I . . ."

I couldn't do it. I couldn't! Not after everything. I wasn't going to drag Shona into this. They'd have to think of something else. "There was no one," I said eventually, my cheeks on fire.

Mr. Beeston grabbed my arm, jerking my body like an electric shock. "You're lying! You *have* to tell me. There was someone with you — I know it. Who was it?"

"I can't tell you!" I cried. Tears slipped down my cheeks. "I can't do it! You can't make me."

"Oh, I think you'll find we can," he hissed.

I gulped. "What if I refuse?"

Mr. Beeston twitched slightly. "Then the kraken won't stop until it has destroyed everything in its sight. These waves we're seeing—you know they're just the start of it."

I thought back to what I'd seen: the kraken smashing up Mandy's boat, what it did to the reef, the rocks . . . the whale. But could I really make Shona face it again? Could I betray her like that? It would finish off our friendship forever.

"I—I'll think about it," I stammered.

He swam over to the door. "Don't think for too long, Emily," he said quietly. "Time is an option we don't have."

Now, this is more like it! This is what our vacation was supposed to be like all along. Luxury cruise liner, lounge chairs, swimming pool, free drinks. We're even getting special attention from the crew because of our trauma.

Yeah, it's all great.

Except. Well, except Mom and Dad haven't spoken a word to each other since we were saved. The atmosphere's so cold when they're around, you'd think we were on a cruise to Antarctica. They're so busy ignoring each other, neither of them has even asked how I am. I sometimes wonder if they'd even notice if I disappeared. I'm tempted to try it—but I'm too much of a coward. What if it only confirmed my worst fears—that no one cares about me?

And then there's Emily. Apart from wondering what she's doing here anyway, and not to mention the fact that she happens to be a *mermaid,* I just can't believe I let her put one over me, yet again. OK, and I'm worried about her, too, all right? Just because she hates me doesn't mean I want her dead.

We set sail again soon. They've been trying to get away from here, but there's something wrong with the ship. It keeps going off course for some reason. They're trying to figure it out, and once they do and we're away from here, I'll *never* get a chance to repay her. She'll always have won.

For once, Dad had actually come up with a brilliant plan, and we let it slip away. If only I could find her. Kill two birds with one stone. Get fish girl back AND save our home. Now *that* would be satisfying!

Maybe I could. Who says it's too late?

I'm wandering around the back of the ship trying to think of something when I hear voices. Three people are standing near the lifeboats. One of them's waving her arms in the air, shouting at someone in a Carefree Cruises uniform.

"But why on earth can't you just let it down?" she's yelling. "I know you used one of them to let a family come aboard. We have to get off the ship! I have to find my daughter!"

"Madam, they were in trouble. We couldn't leave them to drown," the Carefree Cruises person replies. "And you won't tell me anything about your daughter's whereabouts. You won't even give me your name. You can hardly expect me to break ship's regulations just because you and your friend here feel like taking a ride in a lifeboat."

The other one looks up. That's when I see who it is. A big woman in a black cape. It's Mystic Millie, the crazy lady who used to read palms on the pier in Brightport! What the—

"A child is in trouble," she says. "That's all you need to know. We've seen things. *I* have seen things. And if you don't mind my saying so, I am rather known for the accuracy of my visions. Isn't that right, Mary Penelope?"

The other woman turns her head as she nods. I duck behind a plastic box full of diving equipment before she can spot me. But I've seen her face. It's Mrs. Windsnap! What are they doing here?

They're moving away. I can't hear the rest of the conversation. But then a thought occurs to me. They want to get off the ship to find Emily. That means she must be nearby.

I could get her! She's probably really near us. Maybe I could get one of those lifeboats myself and find her. Someone's got to do something—and it doesn't look as though Mom and Dad are going to bother. Too busy ignoring each other.

It's not as if they'll even miss me. No one would miss me. And if I get lost at sea, well, they'll be sorry then, won't they.

Before I can talk myself out of it, I'm grabbing everything I'll need—snorkel, mask—and clambering down a ladder that reaches the lifeboats. I *know* it's crazy; I know it is. But what are my options? Stay here being Mandy-no-friends or actually do something with my life? And if I get her, maybe Dad can have his dream after all and save our home. He might even remember who helped him do it. But what about her mom? I'd have to get around her. Well, I'll think of something. I'll have to.

I'm lost in thought—so lost, in fact, that I'm not looking at what I'm doing. Standing on the edge of the lifeboat, fiddling and yanking at ropes and belts, trying to figure out how you release the boats. It's ridiculous. I'd never manage it. The whole plan is ridiculous. Mrs. Windsnap's not going to stand by and watch while I snatch her daughter—if I could even find her. I don't know what I was thinking. I must be losing it.

I'm about to clamber back up to the deck. But as I'm reaching out to grab the ladder, something slips: my hand—I miss the ladder. Then my foot—the ladder's too slippery—I'm falling! No! I lurch out to get hold of the ladder, but it's too late. I miss again, bashing my hand against the ladder and banging my leg as I fall.

With an enormous splash, I land in the sea! HELP!

No one can hear me. The cold jams my brain as the ship speeds away. Oh, God—help!

Then Emily's face comes into my mind and with it a new thought: she's my only hope of getting out of this mess. The only person who might possibly, possibly help me. I need to find her.

I can see all the way to the bottom of the sea. It's incredible: so clear, so blue. Tiny speckled fish, spongy purple and green plants, trees almost. It's a whole other world down here.

There's something else down here, too.

But I'm not thinking about that. I refuse. I can't afford to think about anything—least of all how I got myself into this ridiculous mess.

How can the ship just leave without me? Leave me totally alone? I've *got* to find Emily. She must be around here somewhere. She can't have gotten far— she was in a net. I swim on.

And on.

And on.

The rocky coral is just below me, all furry, as though it's covered in dust and fluff. Pink, gooey, jelly-like clumps clutch at the rocks. A dull gray fish glides toward me. Then suddenly it flaps bright purple fins. It looks like an airplane with fancy painted wings.

Where am I?

I'm exhausted. There's no sign of her anywhere. I tread water while I adjust my mask and look around. The ship's miles away.

There's a plank of wood floating nearby. I've just got enough energy to reach it. It looks like a piece of our boat! My teeth chatter as I cling to it and try to figure out what the heck I'm going to do next.

The water's really dark here, and murky. I dip under to look around, but I can hardly see anything. The jelly stuff seems to be reaching higher, trying to grab me. And there are too many sea urchins.

And then I see something stringy, floating up toward the surface. I paddle over to examine it. It's a piece of net; I'm sure it's hers.

She got away, then.

There's something else. Something very big. Black on top, white underneath, a giant fin on its back. It's coming toward me!

I want to scream. I know I want to scream—but I can't. I can't get anything out of my throat. I couldn't even if I wasn't underwater, in the middle of the sea, miles from anywhere. It's the monster! I knew it! I should have trusted my instincts. I'm an idiot. And now I'm a dead idiot.

Maybe I can get away before it eats me.

But it's not moving.

Yes, it is. But not toward me. It's kind of floating, gliding slowly upward. And it's not the monster.

It's a killer whale. And it's dead.

As it floats past me, I watch with morbid fascination. There's a chunk missing from its side. My body starts to shake.

My legs don't seem to be working anymore. *Please just get me back to the ship! Please get me away from here. I'll do anything. I'll be nice to Mom and Dad; I'll even forgive Emily for everything. Just get me back to the ship alive!* Please!

Something grabs my legs. That's it. I'm dead.

I don't even struggle. I can't. My body feels as useless as the half-eaten whale. I close my eyes and wait for—

"Who are you?"

What? I open my eyes. A man's face has appeared in front of me in the water. Young, almost a boy. He's gripping my arms. Where did he come from?

I open my mouth and swallow about a gallon of water. He waits while I splutter half to death and put my snorkel back on.

"Come with me," he says.

Still holding my elbow with one hand, he pulls me along in the water. I catch a glance under the water as we swim—and that's when I see. He's not a man. He's a merman! He's got a long tail with silver rings all the way down.

We're heading toward something that looks like an island. As we get closer, I realize it's just a collection of rocks and caves. We swim among the rocks.

"Nathiel," the merman calls. Still holding on to me, he yanks me downward. I quickly adjust my snorkel so I can still breathe.

Below us, a rabbit warren of rocks and tunnels and caves spreads out as far as I can see. It's like a city, packed with too many buildings crammed together as closely as possible.

An old guy with a scraggly beard appears from inside a large crevice. Another merman! We come back up to the surface together.

"Another one?" he says.

"Another what?" I burst out. "Have you got Emily?"

The young merman looks at the older one. "Emily?" he says. "Sharks alive, Nathiel—d'you think this is the one?"

The older merman turns to me. "You're Emily's friend?" he asks.

"I—" What has Emily got to do with this?

"You were looking for her!" he shouts, shaking me.

"Yes!" I burst out. "Yes, I'm looking for Emily. Is she here?"

"Kyle, tell the boss right away," the old merman orders. "Take her to the Lantern Cave first. It's the only safe place above water."

Kyle turns to swim away with me.

"No!"

They both swivel their heads to stare at me.

"Please," I say. A tear streaks down my cheek. I don't care. Anyone would cry in these circumstances. Anyway, I'm not crying. It's the sun. It's shining right into my eyes. "Please let me go home."

"Where's home?" Kyle asks.

Good question. Home. You know, the place that's about to get pulled down, where I live with two people who can't stand the sight of each other.

"I need to get back to my parents. Please." I blub like a baby. Have I really been reduced to this? Begging to be with my parents!

Nathiel says, "And where are they?"

"I don't know."

He turns to Kyle. "Just get her to the Lantern Cave for now. We can always—"

"They're on a ship," I say.

Nathiel snaps back to face me. "What?"

"They're on a ship, over there somewhere." I point back in the direction I think I came from. I sob. I can't help it. "Please let me get back to it."

The pair of them look at each other.

"A ship." Kyle's eyes are shining. "This is it!

First the kraken, now a ship for it. We can get back to work, back to the old days. We need to move fast."

What's he talking about? "Are you going to let me go?" I ask.

Nathiel turns to me, grips my shoulders. "You want to go back to your ship?" he asks.

I nod.

"And you can show us where it is?"

"I—I think so."

Nathiel lets me go. "Handed to us on a plaice," he says, smiling at Kyle. "Good work. We're going to be rich."

Kyle's cheeks flush. He doesn't speak again, just takes me toward a cave. I squeeze through the tiny entrance. It opens out when we get inside. It's dark, and creepy. I can just about make out strange shapes hanging down from the roof. Tiny chinks of light coming through holes way above me, huge boulders with brown gooey stuff that looks like caramel icing dribbled over them.

He closes a barred metal door and locks it from the outside. I grab the bars. "Wait!"

"We'll take care of you," he says, his face cold and expressionless. "Don't worry."

Don't worry, I say to myself as he swims away from me. I climb out of the water onto a rocky ledge, my body shaking and cold. Sure. Absolutely. Why would I worry? I mean, I've only been locked in a dark cave by myself, with nothing but weird clumps of rocks hanging from the ceiling like enormous crooked fingers pointing at me.

I turn away from the pointing fingers. I've got to get out of here. I just need a plan. I'll think of something.

I shiver as the darkness closes around me.

Chapter Eight

I swam around my cell for the hundredth time.
"Let me out!" I yelled, scratching my hands
down the rocky walls. My voice echoed around
me. Finally, I slumped in the corner.

The next thing I knew, the door was rattling. I
leaped up as Mr. Beeston came in carrying a net
basket filled with shellfish and seaweed. He placed
it on a rocky ledge beside me. Water crashed around
me as I reached for it, throwing me against the
sides.

"See that?" he snarled as I grabbed the ledge
to stop myself from being thrown back against the
wall. "That's virtually constant now. And it'll keep
getting worse, until you've done what you need
to do."

I didn't reply.

"Eat your breakfast," he said, nudging a finger at the basket. "You need to be strong."

"I don't have to do what you say." The edges of my eyes stung.

"Really? Well, you won't be interested in our new visitor, then. Kyle tells me he's found someone who might make you feel differently."

"A visitor?"

"A friend."

I quickly rubbed my eyes. "You've got her here? But how did you know—"

"Eat up quickly," he growled in a voice that made my skin itch. "It's time for a reunion."

We swam up toward the surface, Mr. Beeston's hand gripping my wrist so tightly it burned. The water grew lighter and warmer as we made our way along tunnels and out into clear water. He pulled me down under a clump of rocks, scattering a group of striped triggerfish. A metal gate filled a gap between the rocks.

"Up there," he said.

My heart thudded. I was really going to see Shona! But what if she wouldn't speak to me after everything that had happened? She'd probably hate me even more now, for dragging her into it again. I had to explain. "Can I see her on my own?" I asked.

"What for?"

"It's personal."

"Ah, friendship, so sweet," Mr. Beeston snarled, his throat gurgling into a laugh. He gripped my arm, his broken nails scratching my skin. "You can have five minutes," he said. Then he fiddled with a lock, and the gate bounced open. I swam through it, along a narrow crack. "And don't try anything smart," he called through the bars.

"I won't."

I swam all the way up to the surface. I was inside a cave, in a tiny pool. Gray pillars lined the edges, their reflections somber in the greeny blue water. A tiny shaft of sun lit up the stalactites hanging from the ceiling like frozen strands of spaghetti. Where was she?

I swam between the pillars, where the pool opened out. Slimy brown rocks lay all around. Thick clusters like bunches of candles protruded upward from the water, black, as though they'd been singed.

"Shona?" I called.

And then I saw her. Sitting on one of the rocks, her back to me.

But it wasn't Shona.

Her hair was short and black. She turned around. For a moment, she looked shocked. Then she forced her angular face into a twisted smile.

"Hi there, fish girl," she said. There was a smug look on her face, but I was pretty sure her voice wobbled a little. "Long time no see."

"Mandy!"

"Having fun?" she asked with a smile.

"Having *fun*? You think being captured and locked in an underwater tunnel is *likely* to be my idea of fun?"

"Oh, sorry. I didn't realize." Mandy examined her nails.

"Didn't realize what?"

"That they didn't like you as much as me. Should have guessed, though. I mean, people never do, do they?"

"What are you talking about?" I gasped.

"Oh, aren't they looking after you nicely? Haven't they promised to take you home?" She glanced at my face. "Oops. Obviously not. Sorry. I always seem to say really hurtful things, *totally* by accident! Don't worry. You can't help it if people don't like you, can you?"

"Yeah, right, Mandy. I don't think so," I said, clenching my hands into tight fists.

"Whatever." Mandy picked up a stone and

threw it into the water. I watched the ripples grow wider and more faint. Then she stepped back up the rock and twirled around the pillars, prancing around the place as though she owned it.

"Why would they like you?"

She stopped prancing and glared at me, eyes wide open and innocent. "What's not to like?"

"Where do you want me to start?" I spluttered.

Mandy frowned. "Anyway, they're stupid," she said quickly. Then she turned to look at me. "Hey, that's a point. *They're* stupid and so are you. Isn't that funny? You'd think you'd get along better, having something in common like that. Anyway, I don't care. They're taking me back to the boat soon."

"Your boat? You didn't sink?"

"Not that old washed-out lump of tin." She laughed. "No, our new boat. Oh, did I forget to mention that we got saved by a luxury cruise liner? Funny enough, they want to treat us like royalty, too! A shame, isn't it?"

"A cruise liner?" My voice suddenly shook. "What cruise liner?"

"The one that we should have been on in the first place. The vacation we were *destined* to have. But not to worry. It's all OK now. They're taking me back later today."

"Taking you back? But why?"

Mandy bit her lip before turning away. "Told you. They like me."

"Mandy, you can't trust these—"

A sound of metal on metal clanked below me. Mr. Beeston appeared. "Five minutes is up."

"Why are you taking her to the ship?" I demanded.

"Think we want to be poor forever?" he asked, adding, "Anyway, we're going together."

"Why? What do you mean about being poor? What aren't you telling me?"

"You know all you need to know," he said. "Let's go."

"That's not her!" I yelled, pointing at Mandy. "*She's* not my friend!"

Mr. Beeston glanced across at Mandy as she turned around. Seeing her face for the first time, he suddenly faltered. "But that's—but you're—"

"*You!*" Mandy spluttered, looking up to notice him for the first time too. "Mr. Beeston. From Brightport! Does someone want to tell me what's going—"

Just then, a huge wave rushed into the cave, filling it almost to the ceiling. Mandy lost her footing and slipped into the water beside me. I grabbed her.

"Get your hands off me, fish girl," she spat. "I can look after myself!"

"No, you can't. You don't know what you're involved in!" I shouted.

Mr. Beeston had disappeared under the water. A moment later, he resurfaced, fighting his way back up against the tide. I turned to face him. "I'm not doing anything for you till you tell me exactly what's going on."

"Want to bet?" he replied. Mandy opened her mouth to speak, but a wave washed her words away. She spluttered and swam for the edge of the pool. Mr. Beeston lunged toward me, grabbing my arm. I tried to struggle, but he tightened his grip, his fingers scorching into my flesh as he pulled me back toward the grille at the bottom of the cave.

Mandy was shouting something as Mr. Beeston pushed me out, fighting against the raging water. I couldn't hear her words anymore.

"What are you doing with me?" I cried as a wall of white water rushed toward us, flinging me against a wall. "What's going on? Tell me!"

"Don't you understand?" he shouted. "We're *all* in danger here. Look at this. We can't live like this. You're the only one who can fix it." We'd reached my cell. He yanked on my arm, pushing me inside. "And you *will!*"

Without another word, he turned and left. I heard the bolt slam across the door.

I slumped back against the wall and closed my eyes. How had it come to this? All I'd wanted to do was fit in. How had I managed to cause such devastation? I looked around my dark cell. Shadows came and went on the walls as the hours passed and daylight faded, along with my hopes.

"Emily?"

Who was that? It sounded like . . .

"Emily!"

Dad? I swam to the door. *"Dad!"* I screamed.

The door burst open. It was! It was him. He wrapped me in his arms.

"How did you find me?" I asked, pressing into his chest.

"I—"

"Wait!" I pulled away from the door as I heard a noise outside. "There's someone out there," I whispered. "How did you get past them?"

Dad took hold of my hands. "Emily," he said in a tight voice. He wouldn't meet my eyes.

"What? What is it?"

"They know I'm here."

"They know? But how—"

"Archie," Dad said simply. "I had to tell, Em. You knew that." He looked briefly at my face and turned away again. He let go of my hands and swam around the cell. "Mr. Beeston came soon after," he continued. He ran a hand through his hair, pulling at it as he struggled to speak. Eventually, he looked up at me. "He told me you hadn't been on your own."

Suddenly it clicked. I felt as though he'd punched me. "So that's why you're here," I said. "You just want me to tell you who I was with."

Dad looked down. "We have no choice, Em."

My throat ached. He hadn't tracked me down, after all. He only came because he had to. Well, I didn't blame him. Why would he want me back after what I'd done?

Dad swam back toward me. "Emily, I *begged* Archie to let me come. He wanted to do it himself."

I didn't say anything. I couldn't. Lifting my chin, Dad spoke almost roughly. "Remember when you found me at the prison?"

I nodded, gulping a tear away.

"That was the happiest day of my whole life," he said. "Did you know that? And you know what was the worst?"

I shook my head.

"The day I thought I'd lost you again."

I held his eyes for a moment before falling back against him. "Oh, Dad. It's been so awful!" I cried. "They want me to face the kraken again."

181

"I know, little 'un, I know." He held me tight while I sobbed. "I'll be there."

"But you won't! I've got to do it on my own."

"Not on your own, Emily," he said, his voice stern. "You weren't on your own." He spoke slowly and deliberately. "You have to tell. You don't know what it's been like at the island. Typhoons, giant waves. One side's totally devastated. All the trees knocked flat. Ships have come off their moorings, and it's only going to get worse."

"It was Shona," I said eventually. I squeezed him tighter. Closing my eyes, I prayed I hadn't just killed off any last chance of her ever making up with me. I couldn't bear to lose her forever; I just couldn't bear it.

Dad swallowed hard. "There's something else I've got to tell you." He held me away from him and picked up both of my hands. "It's your mom and Millie. They went out looking for you, and we can't find them. There's folk out searching and I'm sure it won't be—"

"Dad! I know where they are."

He jerked backward. "What?"

"I've seen them." I told him about everything: the ship, Mandy, Mr. Beeston.

Dad listened with wild eyes. "Emily, there's no time to waste," he gasped when I'd finished.

"We've got to do this. I'll send a message to Archie."

"Don't leave me!" I gripped his arm. I couldn't be left alone again now. I couldn't lose Dad again. Please no!

"I'm not going anywhere," he said firmly. "I'll be by your side the whole time."

"Do I really have to do this?" I asked, my voice quivering.

Dad held me close as he spoke into my hair. "I'm sorry, Emily. It's the only way."

That creepy Mr. Beeston's pulling me along through the water on a kind of raft. I *never* liked him, back at Brightport. He's even worse now. He keeps shouting things to me. "Where's the ship?" he bellows.

"I—I think it's—"

"WHERE'S THE SHIP!" he repeats, about ten times louder.

"It must have moved," I call back to him. "It was somewhere over there." I point vaguely ahead of us.

"You know nothing, child," he says. "I don't know why we even brought you. No matter, we'll find it soon. It's probably already there."

"Already where?" Emily calls. She's here too, with another merman. I think it's her dad. They keep smiling at each other. Lucky them. My chest aches as I wonder if I'll ever get to smile at my dad again.

"The edge of the Triangle. Same place we're heading."

"You have to *tell* me!" Emily's screaming. "*Why* do you need the ship?"

"We're just getting our bearings," Mr. Beeston says.

Emily turns to the other merman. "He's not telling us everything," she whimpers. "I *know* he's not. Why would they be taking Mandy home? It doesn't make sense."

"Shh, just let's get there. We want your mom back. This is our best chance," he replies in a quiet voice, glancing nervously at Mr. Beeston. What are they up to? "It'll be OK," he says, holding Emily's hand. "I'm here to take care of you."

We swim on. I keep having visions of seeing Mom and Dad again. *Please get me to the boat. I promise I'll change. I won't be horrible anymore.*

The water breaks in sharp waves all around us. It's getting really rough as we plow through enormous peaks and crash down into huge troughs. I'm grabbing the side of my raft, totally soaked.

And then I see it.

In the distance. On the horizon. I think it might be portholes, glinting in the sunlight. Yes, it is! A whole row of them! It's the ship!

"That's it!" I shout. "Over there!" I point to the right.

We speed toward the cruise ship. I'm going to see Mom and Dad again! I'm going to be safe!

As we get closer, I can see its shape more clearly. And then it goes out of sight. There's something in

185

the water, in front of the ship. It's like an island; a sickly khaki-green island with hills and bumps. And it's moving. Long arms reaching up, propelling it forward, blotting out the sun. I grip hard onto the raft as my stomach turns over.

The monster's going to get the ship.

I realize I'm screaming.

"Mandy, I can stop this!" Emily yells to me. "They've told me I can calm it."

"Why should I believe you?" I shout back. "You think you're so special, don't you? Think you can do everything better than anyone else!" Tears are streaming down my face. Mom, Dad. They're so near and I'll never see them again.

"Listen to me!"

"No! I *won't* listen to you. If I hadn't been trying to find you, none of this would have happened! It's all your fault! Every single thing that's gone wrong here is YOUR FAULT!"

Emily doesn't speak again. Her face looks like it's been slammed between two walls. I force myself not to look, not to care.

Why should I care? No one cares about *me*.

I'm going to die out here, and absolutely no one cares.

186

Chapter Nine

I gulped as we swam, trying to swallow, trying to breathe. Trying not to think about what I had to do.

Could I really calm the kraken's rage? Did I have any choice?

We were getting nearer to the ship—and so was the kraken. The thought of Mom on the ship was all I needed to spur me on. I *had* to do it.

"Look!" Dad pointed at two shapes in the water. Archie and Shona!

Archie swam up to Mr. Beeston, pulling Shona along with him. "We've got her," he said simply.

Mr. Beeston nodded curtly. "Just in time."

Shona! Excitement bubbled inside me—but quickly turned to ice when I saw her face. She wouldn't meet my eyes. Well, I didn't blame her. After everything I'd put her through, now she had to come face to face with the kraken again, and it was thanks to me—again. I fought back tears.

Archie looked across at me. "I'm glad you're safe," he said, trying to smile.

"Safe? What makes you think I'm safe?"

"Come on. We don't have any time to lose." He started swimming again, Shona joining Mandy and me as we trailed along behind the others. Dad swam up ahead with Archie.

"I'm not surprised you're not speaking to me," I said, building up the courage to speak to her as we sliced through the water. *Please don't ignore me, please!*

Shona looked at me through heavy eyes. "What d'you mean?" she asked. "I thought you wouldn't be talking to me! I was so horrible to you. I've been a coward and a terrible friend. I wouldn't be surprised if you never want to speak to me again."

I grabbed her hand as we swam. "Shona, you weren't a terrible friend! If anyone was a terrible friend, it was *me*. I dragged you somewhere you didn't want to go."

Shona squeezed my hand. "I should never have let you take the blame. I'm so sorry," she said. Then more quietly, she added, "And so are Althea and Marina."

"Althea and Marina? Your new best friends, you mean?"

Shona laughed. "My what? Why would I want them when I've got the best best friend in the world?"

I held my breath. "You mean . . . ?"

"Yes!" She grinned. "I mean you! I mean a best friend who's crazy and impossible and maddening and strong and brave." She held my eyes. "And unique," she added.

My cheeks burned. "You do?" I gulped.

Shona nodded. "I was just too stubborn and stupid to realize it for a while. And you know, Althea and Marina want to be friends with you too," she added. "They feel awful about taking us to the lagoon. They think it's all their fault. They wanted me to tell you they're going to make it up to you at the welcome party, when we get back."

The welcome party. Were they still really going to hold a welcome party for us? Would I really ever be truly welcome there?

"Well, excuse me for not joining in the happy moment," Mandy burst in, "but does either of you realize we're all about to *die* out here? Shouldn't we be trying to get *out* of this mess?"

"Mandy's right," I said, suddenly realizing Mandy and Shona had never met. Somehow, this didn't feel like the best time for introductions. "We need to think about what we're doing."

Ahead of us, the kraken had dipped under-water, an occasional tentacle lashing out across the surface. The sea bubbled with expectation.

Shona turned to me. "What *are* we doing?"

That was a very good question.

We were there. The edge of the Triangle; the realm of the kraken. It was no longer a glassy plane over the ocean. An endless chasm stretched across the sea, giant waterfalls tearing down into the blackness below.

The ocean raged as the kraken surfaced in front of the chasm. Huge tentacles surged out of the sea, thick and lumpy, spraying water all around as they crashed onto the surface again and again.

I froze.

I couldn't do it.

Someone was shouting at me. I think it was Archie. It could have been Mr. Beeston, or even my dad. It didn't matter. I couldn't change this, I couldn't face the kraken. I closed my eyes.

"The ship." Mandy was pulling at my arm. "The ship," she said over and over again. "It's going to sink the ship! *Do* something!"

The monster was looming over the ship as it edged toward the chasm. Tentacles reached high into the air. One swipe and it would all be over. "MOM!" I screamed into the wildness, my eyes blurred from tears and seawater.

Archie grabbed my arm. "Face it!" he screamed. "Both of you!"

"*Then* what?" Shona cried.

"Just do it! Face it together and be silent. Wait till it turns this way. I'll tell you what to do then. Quick!"

Shona turned to me.

"Come on," I said. "It'll be OK."

I grabbed her hand and we turned to face the kraken together, waiting in silence for the awful moment when it would turn that long, hard, horrible face toward us.

And then it did.

Nothing else moved. The sea swells stopped. The crashing waves leading down into blackness, the chasm — everything was still, held in a freeze frame. The kraken stood like a terrifying statue, motionless like iron, a giant tentacle poised over the ship, its bulging, weeping eyes locked with ours.

"It's working," Dad whispered into the stillness. "It's working!"

In the distance, a chariot was gliding over the water, pulled by dolphins. Neptune was on his way.

Archie glanced across at the chariot. "You have to do it now!" he urged. "Bring the kraken here, calm it down. Now!"

"What do we do?"

"Think."

"Think?"

"In your minds, try to communicate with it."

"*Communicate* with it?"

"Try to hold it in your power, bring it out of its rage so it can return to Neptune. You have to move fast."

"OK." I pulled at my hair, twirling it around as I flicked my tail. I glanced at Shona. She nodded quickly. OK. I just have to calm the kraken's rage. Think thoughts.

OK.

Calm down, nice kraken. I forced the words into my mind, my face squirming up with disgust and horror. A tentacle twitched, lashing out into thin air.

"You have to really feel it," Archie said. "It's no use pretending. It'll know."

Neptune was coming closer. I had to do something before he got here, prove that I wasn't completely and utterly useless, that I hadn't ruined absolutely everything. Shona's eyes were closed, her face calm and focused. OK, I could do this.

Please, I thought. *Please don't destroy anything. There's no need. Take it calmly, listen to us, trust us, it's all OK. No one's going to hurt you.*

Random thoughts raced through my head, anything I could think of that might have some effect.

And it did—it started to. The kraken's tentacles were softening, flopping back down onto the water, one by one. The swell of the sea had started shifting slowly, rising and falling steadily, the huge choppy waves with their sharp crests smoothing into deep swells. The chasm closed over, lying shiny and smooth like an oil slick.

"Good!" Mr. Beeston called. "Keep doing it!"

Don't be angry. Everything will be all right. Just be calm, calm, calm.

Beside me, I could almost feel Shona's thoughts, the same as mine, weaving in between my own words. The kraken was calming down. Its tentacles lay still and quiet, spread out across the ocean's surface.

The chariot was coming closer. I could see Neptune, rising out of his seat, holding his trident in the air.

"We've done it," he cried as the dolphins

brought him to my side. "Bring it here. Bring it to me now. Only when it is right in front of you can you bring it fully back into my power."

I swallowed. Here? Right in front of us?

"Now!" Neptune repeated.

I cleared my throat as I glanced at Shona again. Her face was white, her eyes wide and terrified.

I closed my eyes. *Come to us,* I thought, half of me praying it wouldn't work, the other half knowing that if it didn't we were all lost.

Nothing happened.

"You have to *mean* it!" Archie said. "I've *told* you that."

I took a deep breath and closed my eyes. Then, forcing myself to concentrate totally on my thoughts, I let the words come into my mind. *Come to us, now. We can end this. No more rage, just calm . . . come to us now.*

Something was happening in the water. Movement. I could sense it. I kept my eyes closed. *It's all right,* I said in my mind. *No one's going to hurt you. Just come to us now and we can work it out. Calm. Stay calm.*

"You're doing well," Neptune said. His voice sounded as though he was talking right into my ear. "Now, open your eyes. You have to come face to face with it, both of you. You need to hold it with your minds until the rage has completely gone."

"How will we know when the rage has gone?" I asked.

"It will come back to me."

I counted slowly to three, and then opened my eyes. It was all I could do not to scream at the top of my lungs. It was there! In front of me! A face as tall as an apartment building: lumpy and dark and pocked with holes and warts, tapering toward huge white eyes streaked with blood-red veins. Enormous craggy tusks pointed up, disappearing into the clouds, it seemed. Tentacles lay still all around it, like a deflated parachute.

I could hear cheering coming from the ship! The danger had passed. We'd done it. We'd really done it! I grabbed Shona's arm. She was laughing.

"We're not finished!" Neptune barked. "Beeston, get ready. Archie, ready?"

"Yes, Your Majesty," Archie replied, swimming away from me.

"Ready for what?" I asked. No one answered. Mr. Beeston and Archie were swimming toward the ship. I grabbed Dad. "Ready for what?" I asked again. "What's going on?"

Dad shook his head. "I don't—"

"What do you think?" Neptune growled. "It's time to put it back to work."

A queasy feeling stirred inside me. Something wasn't right.

"You don't think this is all merely to save your lives, do you?" Neptune asked. "Don't you think there is more to my kingdom than that?"

"I—I don't know. I don't under—"

"The kraken is getting back to work, as I've told you. It's been nearly a hundred years, and now it will return to what it knows best: relieving humans of what they do not need. It will bring me riches in quantities I haven't known for many years."

What did he mean? He couldn't possibly—

"And that"—he pointed to the ship—"is where we start."

"But you can't!" I yelled. The kraken stirred as I shouted, a tentacle hitting the water with a splash that covered us all. "You tricked us! You made us do all this, just so you can destroy everything!"

Mr. Beeston turned in the water. "We're not going to destroy everything. That's what the kraken would have done without you. We want to regain the control that is rightfully ours."

"And the riches," Neptune added, stroking a gold sash around his chest.

"Exactly, Your Majesty," Mr. Beeston added with a creepy smile.

"Why didn't you just let it sink the ship, then?" Shona asked.

"It will sink it for *me*! When *I* am ready. Otherwise, it is wanton destruction."

"Wanton destruction?" I spluttered. "And this isn't?"

Neptune's face bulged red. "Without me, the kraken will destroy everything in its sight, losing it forever into the chasm. I will *not* suffer that waste!" He waved his trident in the air. "Now go to it! I want every jewel from that ship!"

"But you'll kill them all!" I screamed, tears streaming down my face. "My mom's on that ship!"

"Did we ASK her to be there?" Neptune boomed. "Did we ASK you to start this?"

"But you can't just *kill* her! And Millie—all of them!"

Mr. Beeston looked at Neptune, then me. "Your mother's on the ship? What the—"

"I want my mom!" Mandy was crying next to me. "I want to go home."

"You can't!" I screamed at Neptune. "Make it not happen—it can't be happening."

The kraken twitched in the water, lifting a tentacle, tipping its head to the side.

"DO NOT lose it!" Neptune bellowed at Mr.

Beeston. "We're too close. It's getting confused. We mustn't lose it now. Beeston, we need to sort this out."

"Please don't do it!" I cried uselessly.

Mr. Beeston wouldn't look at me as he set off toward the ship. "I'm sorry, Emily," he said.

Dad lunged after him, grabbing his arm. "My WIFE is on that boat!" he screamed.

Mr. Beeston's left eye twitched. "That—it's not our concern," he stammered.

"Not your concern? Don't you care that people are going to die when you sink their boat?"

"Tough tails!" Mr. Beeston suddenly exploded. "They shouldn't stray into Neptune's kingdom. He is the ruler; everything in the ocean is his. He is only regaining what he's owed. Humans have stolen from him for centuries, poaching his seas for their own needs. We're just redressing the balance."

He was crazy. They all were.

Something was happening in the water. The kraken's tentacles were twitching, batting the water, spraying us all.

"OBEY ME!" Neptune screamed. "It's caught between your control and mine. We have to combine them or it will go insane."

"We won't!" I yelled back. "We WON'T obey you!"

I grabbed Shona and Mandy. "Come on!"

Mandy pulled away from me. "Look what you're doing!" she shouted. "You're making it *worse!*"

She was right; the kraken was coming back to life, tentacles rising to smash against the water.

"It's going to kill *everyone!*" Mandy yelled. "You have to stop it!"

"Then what? If we obey Neptune, it'll go back into his power again, and he'll make it sink the ship anyway!" I cried. "What can we do?"

It was ahead of us. Mr. Beeston was calling it to the ship. No!

The kraken lashed forward, tearing a hole through the sea as it spun toward the ship. The Triangle's surface was opening up again!

And then. And then.

I saw it in slow motion.

A tentacle, rising into the air, water spiraling off around it in an arc of color and light. It came crashing down onto the water, hitting out, thwacking at the surface, swiping at the ship. The ship! It was so close. I could see people lined up along the decks, running madly, but there was nowhere to run. The tentacles rained down. It had the ship! It knocked at it, hungry for destruction. The ship was tilting, people tossed from the deck—hundreds of people in the water, screaming for their lives.

"MOM!"

I whirled toward the kraken, edging toward the chasm; I could feel it pulling me—something holding us together; I couldn't fight it.

For a split second, everything stopped. The calm came back. The kraken had disappeared under the water. In silence, I watched the chasm close up, covered over again with the glassy surface of the sea.

Just one brief moment of calm, before a screeching wail split the air around us. Lights flared. The glassy surface splintered and cracked. The whirling sea raged below. And the kraken rose. It burst through the water, screaming up from deep below the surface, its long face stretched wide by angry, gaping jaws exposing daggerlike teeth as its tentacles scrambled madly like a mass of giant maggots, smashing the still surface of the sea. As we watched, the water fell away, pouring like a waterfall, leaving just the kraken, surrounded in its fury by utter, black emptiness.

"We've lost our power," I said feebly to no one. "It's not listening."

I was being dragged toward the kraken. I could feel its mind pulling me toward it. Nothing I could do.

I couldn't save anyone. This force pulling me was too strong. No energy, no power to do anything.

I let myself slip toward the chasm.
And it closed behind me.

Down, down, into complete darkness. Nothing to see. No water, no land. Nothing. Falling through nothingness. Spiraling down, whisked around in a vacuum of whirling blackness, twisting me, throwing me around and around.

It grabbed me.

Lashing at me, scorching my face, my hands, my body, the kraken's tentacles screamed across me, again and again. I writhed and struggled, but it was impossible. I couldn't keep out of its clutches.

I touched something that felt like jelly. With shuddering, horrified disgust, I realized it was the edge of a sucker the size of a dinner plate. I gripped my body, trying to curl into a tight ball of nothingness.

"Why are you doing this?" I shouted uselessly as sticky, slippery tentacles slithered across my body, creeping around my tail, around and around, pulling me into a locked coil. I couldn't move a single thing. Brown hairs brushed across my face, writhing like a nest of worms. Terror sucked my breath away.

What could I do to stop it? Beg? What could I say? Why wasn't it *listening*? I'd woken it up! It should be in my power!

My thoughts rambled uselessly as tears streaked down my cheeks.

The tentacles reached higher and tighter, wrapping me up, trapping my arms, climbing up my body, finally closing around my neck.

This was it. This was where it ended. No one to save me.

The darkness slowly grew darker.

The ship's safe! It's all stopped. The monster's gone. But the people are still in the water. Lots of them. Someone's got to save them.

"What have you done with her?" Emily's dad is screaming at the really tall merman in the throne. "What have you done with her? Give me my *daughter*!"

The big merman waves this great big fork thing around. "Do you DARE question me in this manner?" he yells at the top of his voice. What is his *problem*? Can't he see people are in *trouble* here?

"Give her back to me!" Emily's dad howls, his voice cracking. "Give her *back*!"

"We can't," the big merman answers. "The kraken has her."

There's uproar after this. The merman's yelling. Some of the people from the ship have broken away. They're swimming toward us, shouting, calling things. They're coming closer.

"MANDY!"

It's Mom! My mom's in the water! I try to paddle my raft toward her. I can't get away. Mr. Beeston's tied it up to that stupid chariot thing.

"Mom!"

What if that massive hole opens up again? What if it sucks us *all* in?

Someone's calling Mom from one of the lifeboats. She hovers in between us.

"Get in the boat!" I yell.

"Stay there, Mandy!" she shouts to me, swimming back to help the others. "I'll get them to come for you."

I nod, swallowing hard as I cling to my raft.

I can't stop thinking about Emily, in there with that thing. I can't let it happen. Was she honestly that bad? What did she ever really do to me?

Maybe I was wrong. Maybe she never had it in for me. It was always me who had it in for her. It was me who tripped her up in swimming, and called her names and stole her best friend. What did she do wrong, exactly? So a few people liked her more than they liked me. Could I really blame them? *I* like her more than I like me at times.

I edge toward the big merman in the chariot.

"Please," I beg. "You have to do something. She's going to die in there."

He turns slowly around toward me, looking down on me as though I'm an ugly beetle that's just crawled out of the sea. "What am I expected to do about that?" he says, his eyes flickering toward the chasm. He looks away from me. "I didn't cause it. She brought it on herself."

"But can't you end it? Make the monster stop?"

"I cannot and I WILL not. Now leave me al—"

"HOW DARE YOU!" Someone suddenly shouts from the other side of the chariot. "Give me a leg up, will you, Jake," she says in a quieter voice to Emily's dad. Then she hauls herself up onto the chariot. Millie! It's Mystic Millie!

The merman glares at her. "Don't you know who I am?" he asks, his voice rumbling like an approaching typhoon.

"Yes, of course. You're Neptune," she says. "But that—"

"KING Neptune!" he booms.

Millie presses her lips together, sucking on her teeth. "Look, you could be King Kong for all I care," she says, squeezing out her long black skirt over the sea. "That still doesn't give you the right to let a poor innocent child get eaten by your precious monster." She stares into his eyes and pulls something out from under her cape. It looks like a gold pendant. "Now are you going to do something about it?" she asks in a low drawl.

He stares back, his eyes flicking to the pendant. No one says anything. As he glares at her, something changes in his eyes. It's as though a flame starts to flicker behind them.

"Well, I . . . ," he says.

Millie moves closer to him. "You know, even the greatest among us are allowed to change our ways if we want to," she says quietly.

Then there's splashing in the water behind me.

"Mandy!"

It's Dad!

He's panting hard. He grabs me, clutching onto the raft. "Thank God," he says. "Thank God." He's crying. I've *never* seen my dad cry. "We've got to do something," he says, his words coming out in rasps. "Too many people in the water—not enough boats—someone's got to help."

"Where's my *wife*?" Emily's dad gasps. He reaches up to grab Millie's hand. "Make him do it," he croaks. "Get my daughter back. Promise me!"

Millie folds a hand over his. "We'll get her back, Jake," she says. "I promise."

He dives under the water and heads toward the ship.

I pull away from Dad. "PLEASE!" I scream at Neptune. "There has to be something we can do."

He lifts his fork thing in the air again. "Leave me alone, all of you," he says. "I do not need this. I will make MY decisions. I will NOT be influenced by ANY of you. If I choose to change my mind, it's not because of anything that you have said to me. Do you hear me?"

"Yes, yes, anything!" I scream.

Millie rolls her eyes, slipping her pendant back inside her cape. "Whatever you say," she says with a frown.

"Well, then," says Neptune, "there is one last thing that may calm its rage and release the child. It comes from an ancient rhyme. It has never been used."

"Why not?" I ask.

"Once its magic is invoked, I lose my power over the kraken forever. It will never return to its old ways. It will be a passive, weak shell of its former self." He scowls in disgust.

"But the old days are gone," I say. "Surely you can see that! We can't cause death just to bring you jewels." Then I add more quietly, "Not that you're likely to even find a whole lot of jewels on that ship anyway."

"So your ways are *better,* are they?" he snaps. "Only the guilty die in your world, do they? Only for 'good' reasons?"

"No, but . . ." My voice trails off.

He waves me away. "But I will not stand by and see this happen. You may be right. Perhaps we will find a different way. Let's get that girl out of there."

207

"What's the rhyme?" Millie demands.

Neptune lifts his eyes to the sky.

*"When old hatred's rift is mended,
Thus the kraken's power is ended."*

"That's it?" my dad yells. "A *nursery* rhyme? That's ridiculous! You said you were going to sort it out."

"It's not just a nursery rhyme, you fool!" Neptune bursts out. "The rhyme itself is not the solution."

"Why tell us it, then?" I ask.

Neptune turns his angry eyes to me. "You asked how to mend the situation. The rhyme will do it—but only once its words have been acted upon. Only when the hatred ends, when the rift is mended, will the power of the kraken finally cease. Do I make myself clear?"

For a moment, there's silence, then they're all shouting again. But I move away. Can I do something? *When old hatred's rift is mended.* I've hated Emily Windsnap for years. Maybe I don't have to anymore. I could change this, do something good. Can I?

She communicated with the kraken just with her mind, didn't she? Maybe I can do the same, somehow. I'm going to try it!

I close my eyes and think of Emily, then I force a thought into my mind:

I'm sorry.

I say it over and over again in my thoughts. And then I wait.

Nothing.

What was I expecting? More flashing lights? I should have known nothing would happen. Nothing ever does when I try to do something good.

She's dead. The kraken's killed her. And I never had the chance to say I'm sorry.

I can see her in my mind. A picture from years ago. We used to play on the pier together. We were almost best friends. Why did I let her slip away?

Years of sorrow well into a tight ball, pressing against my throat.

But then—

I forgive you.

What was that? Who said it? I look around. No one's near me. They're all too busy shouting at each other, arguing over where to find the old hatred that they have to mend. I swipe a hand across my cheek, wiping away tears and seawater as I listen hard.

I forgive you.

It's Emily. It's her voice. I can hear her, again and again.

And then the chasm opens. It's starting again. It's whirling, throwing water around everywhere, splashing us all. A giant wave heaves toward us, knocking me off the raft.

"MANDY!" Dad yells, lunging for me. He swims away from the current, grabbing the raft and heaving us both back onto it.

"Please, no!" he sobs. "Don't let me lose you." He holds me tight, clutching my face to his chest as we kneel together on the raft.

When did my dad last hold me like this?

Over his shoulder, I can see the ship—but it's on the other side of the chasm. How will we ever get back to it?

As I stare into the raging water, all thoughts are suddenly swept from my mind. The monster's coming out of the sea again. Its head bursts out through the surface, scratched and veined with black lines, pus oozing out of craterlike holes in its skin. Piercing sounds of agony fill the sky.

Tentacles lash everywhere—it's out of control, screaming, on and on, the screeching siren sound. Roaring with anger, the monster lashes out again and again. And then I notice something in one of its tentacles. Emily! It's got her, holding her tight, throwing her into the air, crashing her back down to the surface. She looks so tiny, like a little doll.

Please don't kill her. . . . She's my friend.

Instantly, one final piercing scream shoots out from the water, exploding like a bomb, sending color and water everywhere.

And it gradually quiets, slows. Stops. The giant waterfall stops raging. It's just a giant hole, spreading and cracking in a line through the ocean.

The monster crashes down onto the water and lies still, tentacles like bumpy highways, bridging the long well, jerking slightly, its head half-sunk in the water. The sea fills with color, purple lights flowing out of the kraken, seeping into the water all around us.

No one speaks. We hover in the sea, in silence, focused on the sight in front of us: the monster lying still, no one moving an inch.

We've done it. We've really done it.

Chapter Ten

J was having the cruelest dream. It started off as a nightmare. The kraken had me. Trapped and half strangled, I was in its clutches under the water. Then I heard a voice: Mandy, apologizing. I thought, *Yes, let's make friends. I'm going to die any second now anyway.*

And then it changed. I was above the water, in the air, thrown high by the kraken. But it let go of me and I came crashing back down onto the water, sinking, then rising back up to the surface.

The worst part was what happened next.

It was the best part really, but so cruel.

I dreamed my mom and dad were there. They'd come to save me. Shona was with them.

We were best friends again. Even Mandy was there, and they were all asking if I was OK. No one was angry with me. All those eyes, looking at me with concern, helping me, carrying me somewhere, forgiving me for all the awful things I'd done. I wanted to call out to them, touch them, but I couldn't move; I couldn't speak.

I can't remember what happened next.

"Emily?"

"She can't hear you."

"She's opening her eyes!"

Mom? I blinked in the sunlight. "Mom? Is that really you?" I asked shakily.

She leaned over me, rocking as she held me tight. "Oh, Emily," she whispered into my neck, her voice choked and raw.

As she pulled away, I rubbed my eyes to see Dad's face next to hers. He was leaning out of the water, reaching up to hold my hand.

Shona was in the water next to him, smiling at me. "You're OK!" she said.

I looked around: gold and jewels beside me, dolphins at the front. I was in Neptune's chariot! And I wasn't on my own. Millie stood at the front, talking in a low, deep voice. I knew that tone. She was hypnotizing someone! But who?

"Now, moving your tentacle very, very slowly, lift another person out of the water," she said softly, "and carry them across the chasm, placing them gently on the deck of the cruise ship. Good, good. . . ."

The kraken was doing what she said.

I shuddered as I remembered being in its clutches, the horror of its tentacles around my neck. . . .

"We did it, then?" I asked numbly.

Shona beamed at me. "You're a heroine, Emily. How could I ever have been angry with you? I'm such a jellyfish at times. Do you realize what you've done?"

"I — no. I don't know."

I knew one thing, though. Whatever I'd done, I hadn't done it on my own. I pulled myself up. "Where's Mandy?"

Shona pointed out to sea. "She's on her way back to the ship," she said. "I think they'll be setting off soon."

I got up, shakily. I had to see her. My legs wobbled.

Mom grabbed my arm. "Emily, you need to rest."

"Later," I said. "I just have to do something."

Before she could stop me, I dived into the sea. I waited for my tail to form. It wobbled and shook just like my legs had, but I could move it. I could get there. I had to see Mandy.

"I'm coming with you, then." Shona swam over to my side.

We made our way toward the edge of the Triangle. I gasped as I saw what lay ahead: a gulf of utter black emptiness. My body shuddered violently as I looked down. Across the chasm, the kraken reached a tentacle from one side to the other and out toward the ship, carrying people carefully across.

"I can't!" Mandy was screaming. "It's HOR-RIBLE!"

"Quick! Come on. It's the only way across." Her dad held his hand out to her. Mandy climbed up onto the awful slimy bridge. My body shuddered. I couldn't go near it!

She tiptoed along the tentacle. It was so huge it almost looked like a road, bridging the emptiness below. By the time I got there, she was nearly across.

"Mandy!"

She turned. The tentacle was starting to slip. Two more steps and she'd be there.

"Emily," she said.

I swallowed. "Thank you."

Two steps away. She paused, stared at me. And then she smiled. I'd never seen her smile before. Not like that anyway. The only smile I'd ever seen from her was a sarcastic sneer. This one suited her better. It looked nice. Made her look like someone I might want to be friends with.

"Yeah, well," she said. "I didn't really do anything."

"No, you're wrong." I smiled back at her. "You did a lot."

Then she lurched across the tentacle, making her way back to the ship.

They'd gone. All of them back on the ship.

As the kraken lay still, I noticed someone in the water beside it. Tall, proud, and silent, Neptune bent forward to stroke a tentacle, holding it sadly. Then he turned and looked around him.

"Beeston!" he called. Mr. Beeston swam toward us from the ship.

"Have you completed the memory wipes?"

"Every last person, Your Majesty."

Neptune nodded. "Good work." Then he clicked his fingers. Instantly, his dolphins squirted water into the air and dived down to pull the chariot through the water. Neptune clambered aboard.

"It's over," he said. "The kraken is falling back into its sleep. Who knows when it will wake now, or if it will even wake at all." He beckoned Mr. Beeston. "We need someone to take on the responsibility of watching over it."

Mr. Beeston's mouth twitched into a crooked smile. "Do you mean . . . ?"

"Who else could I trust with such an important task?"

Neptune looked around at us all. "The rest of you will return to your lives. The kraken keepers will join you at Allpoints Island and you'll live together. The Triangle shall be sealed when I have left. Now, back to your island, everybody, and try to keep out of trouble this time."

The ship was almost out of sight, a silhouette slowly gliding along the horizon.

Dad put an arm around me as Shona caught up with us, linking an arm in mine. Mom and Millie smiled at me from inside the lifeboat.

"Hang on," Mom said. Then she pulled her

dress off. She had her swimsuit on underneath. Pinching her nose, she jumped into the sea and swam over to join me and Dad.

"I've been practicing," she explained simply as we stared.

Dad kissed her, then turned back to me with a wide grin. "Come on then, little 'un." He nodded toward Allpoints Island as he pulled me close. "Ready to go home?"

Home. I thought about our bay, about *Fortuna*, Barracuda Point, the Grand Caves, mermaid school, the million things I hadn't yet discovered about Allpoints Island—and everyone waiting for us. Althea and Marina, and all my other new friends.

"Yes, I'm ready," I said eventually. Then I turned to Shona and smiled. "We've got a party to go to."

LOCAL HEROES SAVE BRIGHTPORT PIER

The Brightport Town Council voted today to retain and modernize the town's historic pier. The decision came after local residents Jack and Maureen Rushton made a substantial donation from a recent windfall.

The Rushtons came into the money due to their stunning photographs of a raging sea monster on the open ocean. The photographs have been sold to newspapers across the world.

The photographs were taken while the couple was on vacation with Mermaid Tours. Bizarrely, they have no recollection of their vacation. "We were as surprised as anyone when we got the pictures developed," Mrs. Rushton said.

The Rushtons plan to expand their amusement arcade on the pier and are currently in negotiations with planners about a theme park, which they will open later this year. The star ride will be a massive roller coaster with a multitude of twists and turns along tentaclelike tracks.

The ride is to be called the Kraken.

ACKNOWLEDGMENTS

Once again, I can't claim to have done this all on my own. Lots of people have been involved in the process. I would especially like to thank:

Jeanette, Andrew, Alex, and Amber, for two incredible weeks in Bermuda;

Ben and Sam, for the day out on the pirate ship (even if it didn't go anywhere);

Fiz, for sharing so many special moments, and crying at most of them;

Kirsty, for being so proud and excited, and so good at sharing champagne;

Fiona and the fab team at Orion Children's Books, for being so behind Emily;

Sarah, for all the beautiful artwork;

my family, and lots of other friends, for all sorts of help along the way.

With extra special thanks to:

Kath, for 100 percent spot-on editorial feedback and for sharing the agony of second-book syndrome;

Lee, for again being a complete inspiration and a central part of helping this book to take shape;

Catherine, for doing all the right things for Emily and for me, and doing them with patience, friendship, care, and skill;

and Judith, for being such a thorough and brilliant editor that all my writer friends are jealous.

LIZ KESSLER is the author of the Emily Windsnap series, including *The Tail of Emily Windsnap, Emily Windsnap and the Monster from the Deep, Emily Windsnap and the Castle in the Mist,* and *Emily Windsnap and the Siren's Secret.* She is also the author of *A Year Without Autumn* and the Philippa Fisher series, including *Philippa Fisher's Fairy Godsister, Philippa Fisher and the Dream-Maker's Daughter,* and *Philippa Fisher and the Fairy's Promise.* She got the idea for the kraken from the name of an amusement park ride, then went on a snorkeling trip to Bermuda to fill in more details. Liz Kessler lives in England.

Dive in and read the
New York Times best-selling series!

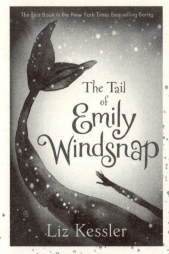

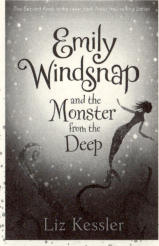

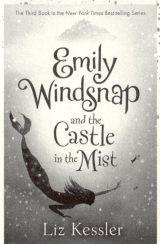

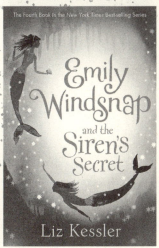

Swimming your way in fall 2012

Emily Windsnap

Four Sparkling
Underwater Adventures!

Watch for the boxed set of all
four titles on the coming tide!

www.candlewick.com

Be a best friend the Emily Windsnap way!

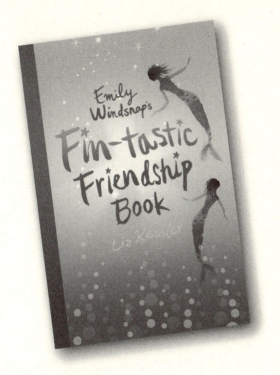

This fanciful friendship book is bubbling with fun activities — perfect for fans of the series to share with their BFFs.

What would you do if you had a fairy godsister?

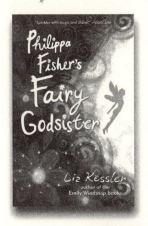

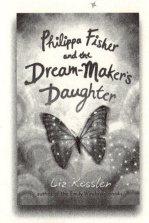

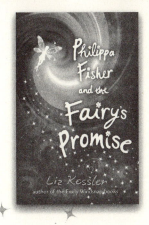